BOTS

BACKWARD CHAINING

Nicole M. Taylor

EPIC
Press

Backward Chaining
Bots: Book #5

Written by Nicole M. Taylor

Copyright © 2016 by Abdo Consulting Group, Inc.

Published by EPIC Press™
PO Box 398166
Minneapolis, MN 55439

Printed in the United States of America.

Cover design by Dorothy Toth
Images for cover art obtained from iStockPhoto.com
Edited by Jennifer Skogen

LIBRARY OF CONGRESS CATALOGING-IN-PUBLICATION DATA

Taylor, Nicole M.
Backward chaining / Nicole M. Taylor.
p. cm. — (Bots ; #5)
Summary: The military Bot program is a shameful failure with Edmond West on the
run. In hiding, Hart's people are creating something different to which the world has
never seen before.
ISBN 978-1-68076-005-7 (hardcover)
1. Robots—Fiction. 2. Robotics—Fiction. 3. Young adult fiction. I. Title.
[Fic]—dc23
2015932715

EPIC
Press

EPICPRESS.COM

"Backward Chaining": *Def. A method of reasoning that involves using a conclusion to reason "backwards" to find available data that might support that conclusion. A common feature of chess game theory as well as computer programming.*

PROLOGUE

MILLON, CALIFORNIA. JUNE, 2047

Wynette knew long before the strange car pulled into the driveway.

It was on every newsfeed: "Rogue roboticist Edmond West dead in Northern California." The details were all over the map. Some news outlets were saying that he'd killed himself, something Wynette considered unlikely. Others suggested that he was slain by his own "people," the synthetic Bots having gotten tired of him, apparently. Wynette, herself, did not speculate. Instead, she cleaned the floors.

In the kitchen, the tile could have used a real re-grouting but she settled for scrubbing in between each tile with the tiny, absurd head of an old electric toothbrush. In the living room, she tired her arms out wiping wide circles on all the windows until they shone. She hung the rugs out on the porch and beat them like they owed her money.

She had not exactly expected the car but, when she saw it, her first thought was: *at least the house is clean.*

Army people—she never knew their names—had visited her right after Edmond went missing. They asked her all sorts of questions about her son and his "known associates" and she assured them that she hadn't been able to predict Edmond's behavior since he was about four years old.

This car was different. There was nothing specifically identifying it as a military vehicle— it looked like an ordinary little Honda, and the people, when they stepped out, weren't wearing uniforms or anything like that. The driver was a petite Black woman with what looked to be a near-permanent frown on her face. The passenger was much taller, an Asian man with a lot of white in his black hair.

The woman looked at the house and then ducked her head back in the car, as if checking against a GPS. "Where you looking for?" Wynette called from the porch, tugging one of the smaller rugs off the railing.

The woman opened her mouth to speak before the man interrupted her: "Are you Wynette West?"

"West is my married name, I go by Graves these days." Wynette answered.

He slammed the car door and headed toward the porch as though Wynette hadn't said anything at all. The woman followed him after a moment.

Wynette gathered the rugs in her arms as they mounted the steps. They stopped just one stair below her, the first deference to her bereavement they'd demonstrated since arriving.

"I suppose you want to come in," she said.

"Please," the woman offered.

Wynette nodded and turned her back to them, nudging open the front door with her elbow.

The two of them stood around awkwardly while Wynette spread the rugs back out on the floor before finally sitting down in the old wing chair that had been her mother's. She'd used it when Edmond was a baby, sitting in it, sleeping in it, waiting next to his crib for the slightest fussing. Edmond was her first and her only, she had always been so nervous with him.

"Take a seat," she said. The two of them awkwardly shared the small sofa across from her chair.

"Ms. West," the woman said, "I'm afraid we have some very bad news."

This wasn't her usual gig, Wynette could see that right away. When Wynette was a girl, her oldest brother had died in Iraq and she would never forget the men who came to tell her father what had happened. They were like wooden carvings, indifferent to sobs, to rage; it felt like all the human softness had been meticulously trained out of them. This woman was uncertain, reluctant. Wynette could have thrown her a line and told her that she already knew about Edmond but she was not inclined, at the moment, to extend any kindness towards these people.

"Your son was killed," the man broke in. The woman pulled a face, so briefly it might have been a mirage, but Wynette had seen it. The woman was used to the man taking charge and talking over her but still it annoyed her.

"A military Bot shot him in the head."

Well. That was clarity, at least.

"We don't know exactly what happened yet," the woman said.

"The Bot defied its orders and its programming." The man gave her a hard look. "It was destroyed immediately afterwards."

He said it as though that mattered to her. Shooting the dog that bit a child didn't unbite the kid, it only made a dead dog.

"We are investigating this incident thoroughly," the woman assured her.

"I'm sure you'll do a fine job," Wynette told her.

There was a little ravel on the right arm of the chair. Wynette picked at it idly with her fingernails.

"You know that we have taken issue with your son and the choices he has made in the past but he was nevertheless a very important part of our team for many years." The man's voice seemed to soften, almost imperceptibly. The woman nodded beside him; it was the first time that the two of them had appeared to be in agreement about anything. "We wanted to come here in person to . . . express that. Our shared bereavement."

Wynette struggled to keep her face neutral. These people had hunted her son to the ends of the earth and now they had the nerve to come here, to her own house and talk as though their grief was in any way comparable to her own. She had birthed that boy, held him in her arms when he was small. She hurt for every hurt he suffered, she soared with his every accomplishment. Losing him was like losing a part of her own goddamn body and she knew already that she would feel the ache and the missing for the rest of her life.

Perhaps the woman sensed a little of what was happening behind Wynette's focused silence because she offered then a very small, "We're sorry. For the part we played in this."

Wynette found it in herself to nod slightly.

"This was the last chance for the Bots program," the man told her. "We are aggressively phasing it out now. The process has already begun. No one else will die the way your son did."

"When will I receive his body?"

The both of them looked startled. Could they not imagine any reason that a mother might want her son's corpse?

"I . . . I'm not sure," the woman looked to the man but, for once, he seemed to have nothing to add to the discussion.

"I'd like to bury my child in a timely fashion."

"Of course," the man said finally, "we'll make sure that happens." His pause was brief, but there was enough time for his demeanor to shift noticeably. He sat taller on Wynette's little sofa, he leaned towards her as though they had established some kind of rapport. "It's going to take a bit of time, though, because we need to do a thorough investigation. Of course, if you have any information to help us, we could probably accelerate that process."

Wynette felt a jolt in her stomach. She couldn't tell if it was a roil of laughter or a spike of nausea. Was he seriously attempting to hold Edmond's dead body hostage? If so, he was about to experience a real disappointment.

"Sorry," Wynette said, "my son quit telling me about his life around the time he started wiping his own ass."

The woman flinched a little but the man didn't even react. *He's probably good at poker*, Wynette thought idly. She wondered how well they had actually known Edmond. Maybe, if she had pried a little bit more, demanded more information, she might know them by sight. Maybe she would recognize the woman as Sarah or the man as Steve. Instead, they were strangers who claimed to have shared something important with her son. She supposed there were a lot of people like that.

Wynette could never pinpoint the moment when Edmond had changed, had transformed from her flesh and blood, her father's nose and her own dark eyes, into someone unlike anyone she had ever known. It was enough to make someone believe in those old stories about fairies carrying off babies and leaving some otherworldly monster behind.

Except that Edmond wasn't terrible, he was wonderful. He wasn't just different than any person Wynette knew, he was better. Smarter, more thoughtful, more ambitious and more genuinely concerned about all the evils of the world.

The older he got, the less it felt as though she had made him and the more it felt as though she'd been gifted with him.

That was why she'd always treated him so delicately. It always seemed to her that he knew what he needed better than she did. But maybe he could have done with a little more in the way of guidance. Maybe.

"We've taken up too much of your time, Ms. Graves," the woman's voice startled them all. It sounded loud as a gunshot in the silence of the house. "We just wanted to express our condolences. On behalf of the military."

Wynette doubted that. The military didn't express "condolences" by taking a seat and chatting with families. They discharged their obligation as quick as possible and got the hell out. They probably still would have done it all by telegram like back in WW II, if they thought they could get away with it.

She realized then that they had never given her

their names and she had not even bothered to ask. Would they have told the truth?

They rose up from the couch in unison. Wynette remained sitting. They knew where the door was. The woman looked like she wanted to say something else but couldn't think of just what that might be. The man looked like he was much more comfortable staring imperiously down at her than looking eye-to-eye. "Edmond was dishonorably discharged several years ago," he said, "but, depending on the results of the investigation, we may be able to reinstate some of his benefits. Of course, as his next of kin, you would receive those."

For several awkward seconds, Wynette struggled to find the words. Finally, she spoke.

"Go fuck yourself."

———o———

Wynette hadn't spoken to Franklin West since Edmond was in high school. When he called that evening, his number showed up as "UNKNOWN" on her flex-tablet. That seemed fitting.

"Hey, Winnie," he said as soon as she picked up. She had the little visual screen blocked, so it was just an audio call. Wynette found herself falling into old habits, listening acutely to his voice to determine how many beers deep he was.

"Are you okay to talk now?" he asked and, to her surprise, he didn't sound drunk at all. And her ear was delicately attuned, capable of discerning the smallest slur, the slightest hesitation, the incrementally slowed speech designed to fool her with watchful precision.

"Yeah," she said, "I'm okay."

"I was just watching the news and . . . " he trailed off, maybe waiting for Wynette to cut him some slack. She took pity on him.

"Yes," she said, "he's dead."

Franklin made a sound like he was choking on something. "Jesus Christ," he said finally.

Wynette couldn't decide what to say next.

Should she comfort him over the loss of a son he had walked away from decades ago? It didn't seem right dragging up all those old hurts right now, though. She didn't think it would help either of them. But damned if she was going to pretend that he lost anything on the order of magnitude of what she had lost.

"How're you holding up?" Franklin asked and Wynette relaxed slightly.

"Okay," she said automatically. "Not so good," she added, after a pause.

"You got anybody coming in to help you?"

"Yeah, my mom is coming down." Wynette's mother had died three years earlier but she didn't want to run the risk of Franklin offering—or worse, insisting upon—assistance. She had managed most of Edmond's life by herself; it felt appropriate now that she should handle his death alone.

"Wynette, I'm sorry." It was a condolence, not an apology, but Wynette accepted it just the same.

Wynette didn't know what to say and it seemed

that Franklin had similarly exhausted his list of conversational topics. Yet, neither of them ended the call and instead they simply waited, listening to one another breathe.

Maybe it was the sound of his breathing that triggered the memory, but Wynette thought suddenly about the day—the night, actually—that Edmond was born. He came almost a month early and they were on their way up from San Diego where they had been visiting Franklin's parents. Wynette started her labor with a dull, squeezing, crushing pain somewhere south of her bellybutton.

Franklin wanted to take her to nearest hospital and Wynette had to grab the wheel to keep him from leaving the freeway. Their scanty little insurance plan only covered a fractional number of doctors and facilities. If they drove off into desert, they would have no idea what they might find nor what it would cost them.

"I can hold on," she had said. Franklin kept flicking his eyes over at her, his whole face drawn together in a stormy pout of worry. She had felt a surge of tenderness for him, even as the contractions seemed to actually be tearing her guts out of her body. "Help me breathe," she told him.

He made a few comical puffing noises, a parody of the kind of Lamaze breathing he might have learned if he'd ever made it to any of those prenatal classes that Wynette had signed them up for.

By Fresno, she felt as though her body was being slowly torn in two. She wondered to herself if all of this was normal. It didn't feel normal, it felt like her muscles were being shredded. She did not say any of this to her husband, who was going ninety in the carpool lane with his hands white on the wheel. "We're okay," she told him, "sometimes labor takes days."

Edmond did not make her wait days. He arrived promptly, forty-three minutes after they got to their hospital. The incredible crescendo of birth seemed to fade from her almost as soon as it was over. Instead, it was the uncertain misery of that long car ride that lingered in her memory. The silence interrupted by heavy breathing and the occasional muffled moan. She had been afraid, despite what she told her husband. The baby was early, the pain didn't feel like any natural hurt she had known. The desert out the window had nothing to offer them save hard dirt and the occasional defeated-looking cluster of adobe houses.

But they made it. All three of them. Franklin covered her hair and her face in kisses; they landed on her skin like sighs. She had loved him so much in that moment but, even then, she demonstrated her love by quarantining all the pain and worry inside herself and never showing it to him. What was it about that man that struck her as so fundamentally fragile?

Why had she ever thought herself so much stronger?

Wynette spoke at last, her voice clear and free from recrimination. "Why didn't you ever try to see him?" she asked. "Once he'd grown up, I mean."

The flex-tab connection was so good that Wynette could actually hear the liquid unsticking sound of Franklin's mouth opening, his tongue moving into position. "I thought . . . if he wanted me in his life, then he would come find me."

It made perfect sense, in his Franklin way. Why make an effort if he could simply wait for someone else to do it for him?

On the other end of the line, someone called out. The voice was distant, far away from wher-ever Franklin was sitting, but Wynette thought it sounded feminine and young.

"Sorry," Franklin said. There was a static-y scrap-ing sound, as though he'd pressed his fingertips against the microphone. His voice, muffled into an indistinguishable murmur, spoke to someone else. "Okay," Franklin said, this time at normal volume.

"Wife?"

"Daughter."

That surprised Wynette, though it probably shouldn't have. She had not kept up with Franklin after the split and she'd done that on purpose, but she had thought about him often over the years. In her mind, he achieved a kind of immortality but a stasis as well. He was always thirty-two and handsome, always putting all his eggs in the most precarious baskets. She knew that he would move on with other women—he was not a man who was built to be alone—but she hadn't expected more children.

A daughter. Edmond had a half-sister. Or he *did* have. Wynette wondered if Franklin had told his little girl anything about her brother or if the two of them were locked away, stuffed back into a corner of his mind like old Christmas decorations in the attic.

"Congratulations," Wynette said, mostly for lack of anything else to say. "Congratulations" was an appropriate response to news of a child and his girl was new to Wynette, if not in general.

"Thank you," Franklin sounded uneasy. "She's twelve."

Edmond had been unexpected even before his unscheduled birth. Wynette hadn't wanted to get pregnant. Her relationship with Franklin was perpetually rocky and she wasn't at all sure that she wanted to have children under the best of circumstances, let alone the ones she found herself in. After he was born, she loved him. She loved him with a kind of elemental savagery that she could scarcely recognize as part of herself, but she also felt certain that Edmond was set apart from all other children and uniquely deserving of that fierce love. Even after Franklin left and Edmond grew up, she did not yearn again for motherhood.

Still, the existence of Franklin's daughter rankled something within her. She wondered if Franklin was still with the girl's mother, if maybe this was his week for visitation. She wondered if this girl had grown to expect so little from her father the way that Edmond had done.

"That's a hard age for a girl," Wynette said. "I hope you treat her right."

It felt mean-spirited, even as she said it. She wouldn't have blamed Franklin for hanging up on her right then.

Instead, he seemed to relax a bit, as though this were something he'd been waiting for all along. "I'm trying," he said, sounding earnest. "Wynette, I've been sober for eleven years now." Well that explained the lack of a slur in his voice. "I know it's too late for most of it, but—"

"Is this some AA thing?" Wynette cut in, "because, if it is, I don't need that." The last thing she wanted to hear was her ex-husband reciting a litany of his failures so he could have the satisfaction of checking off another step off his list.

"That's fair."

He had tried AA several times while they were still married. She remembered driving him to the meetings at the community center and waiting outside in the car, those little packets of chemical hand warmer in her pockets because the heater was broke. It had never seemed to take when he was with her but she supposed the eighth or ninth time must be the charm.

She could have been angry. A few years ago, maybe even a few days ago, she would have been angry to discover that her erstwhile husband who had given so little and taken so much had gone out into the world and started over, fresh and clean and unimpeded by obligation. It would have enraged her that he had the temerity to pull his shit together, transform into a man worth having, for another woman and another child when he could not do that for her and Edmond.

Now, though, she felt nothing but a kind of dull hollowness. It was the same thing she'd felt since she realized that the news feeds were all reporting the same thing, that her only child was dead.

"I'm . . . glad for you," Wynette said. "I really am."

She was made ashamed of her uncharitable thoughts by the genuine, slightly pathetic gratitude in his voice when he answered: "Thank you, Wynette."

———o———

Wynette was used to being alone, ideally she could do it without being lonely. Edmond hadn't been back in years even before his difficulties and her mother had been the last of her family left on the West Coast. She had friends who occasionally went out with her, to the movies or to the bar or to some local event but, overwhelmingly, her nights were spent just like this one, in a silent house in the gathering dark.

Tonight, though, the solitude felt uniquely weighty. She felt a hankering she hadn't experienced in years; she wanted a cigarette. She had quit smoking when Edmond was in high school but very occasionally she would long for the feeling, not just of nicotine rushing her blood but the physical reality of it, clicking the lighter to life, the featherweight between her fingers, raising it to her mouth and lowering it again. There was a ritual to it that always comforted her. She wondered if that was the way Catholics felt about their rosary beads.

That was how she found herself in the upstairs linen closet, tearing through old vacuum sealed bags of winter clothing. There was a big down jacket in there and, if she remembered correctly, half a pack of smokes in the pocket.

She did not pause to examine the hats, the gloves, the jackets that had belonged to her dead son. They passed through her hands like water from a faucet.

She had dug out the old coat—it was near the bottom—and she was just about to dive into the pockets when she heard the knock at the kitchen door. It was soft. If it had been during the bustling daytime, she would not have heard it over ordinary house noise.

Wynette didn't know who it would be at her door—another military goon to strong-arm her?

Franklin, having uncharacteristically decided to help out after all? Some well-intentioned friend who recognized Edmond's name on the news?—but Wynette found she did not care. She dropped the jacket back in the closet and descended the stairs almost mindlessly, as if pulled along with a string.

She opened the door without bothering to peer out the little window in the top and looked down. The boy at the door was maybe four feet tall; he looked about seven years old. He was wearing just a striped t-shirt and dirty jeans and he had a backpack on. He looked up at her with a grave, assured expression that reminded her (with a pain precise and cold as an icicle) of Edmond at that age. The kid didn't look like Edmond—his hair was sandy-blonde instead of dark, straight where Edmond's had been curly, and his eyes were big and green. He was heavily freckled—but there was something in his demeanor that was so familiar she had to stop her arms from reaching out to him.

"A friend sent me," the little boy said. His voice was childish but his words were serious and measured, like an adult man speaking through a voice modulator.

"Your friend or mine?" Wynette asked.

"Both."

"And why did our mutual friend send you?"

"She said that you would look after me."

Wynette relaxed against the doorframe and smiled slightly. It occurred to her that she couldn't actually remember the last time she had smiled. "And why would I do that?"

The boy looked thoughtful. He swung his arms, as though reaching for his backpack. It was the closest he had come to looking his age so far. "Because you need a son," he said.

Wynette had watched her son's career with absolute pride but with little depth. She understood generally what he did and how it was linked to the shiny, plastic-faced machines she saw advertised during movies and television shows, but no one in Millon had actually seen a Bot in the . . . flesh. Except that she had, years and years ago, before Edmond ran. He had brought a young woman to her—the first and last time he had done so. It was not some girlfriend that he wanted her to rubber stamp, though. Wynette had a sense from her at the time, a sense of the . . . supernatural, for lack of a better word. Not like a ghost story or a Halloween ghoul, but something truly outside the natural world and immune to its laws. Edmond had never confirmed anything but Wynette had known long ago that her son had indeed taken the time to show her his masterpiece.

The boy in front of her now gave her the same feeling as that young woman all those years ago. There was something about him that extended beyond human. He was another of Edmond's creations, the closest thing to children that her son would ever have.

Wynette stepped away from the door to let the boy through. "Alright," she said, "do you eat?"

"Sometimes," said the boy.

ONE
DECOMMISSIONED

"**Y**ou will feel different. Don't be alarmed."
Ebert thought that would be virtually impossible but he didn't want to argue with the . . . doctor? Nurse? Scientist? Whatever she was, he figured that she had a tough enough job without getting lip from him.

She was a pert looking woman, her hair shaved close on either side of her head with a long floppy mohawk of brown in the middle. She was wearing a thin white coat, however, and what looked like a uniform underneath it. Military issue, maybe? Not exactly like the ones they had given to Ebert and the other Bots headed to Isla Redondo, but of a similar make. "We were forced to make some modifications to your brain," she continued in that same soothing, upbeat tone. "To remove the kill switch."

Immediately, Ebert's hand flew to the side of his head. He touched the skin above his ear with his flat palm and felt . . . smoothness. Not even the ripple of cut flesh joined together.

"Oh, there won't be any cosmetic defects." The woman puffed her chest out as though she had personally performed his surgery. Perhaps, Ebert thought, she had. "We have some very good craftspeople here."

"Where is *here*?" Ebert thought he should inject the question into the conversation quickly, before she moved on to something else.

For the first time, the woman frowned. "It doesn't have a name," she said, "not yet. We haven't decided."

Ebert rested his head back on the pillow. It was soft and warm from his body heat, slightly moist from what he presumed to be his sleepy breathing.

He closed his eyes and focused on his head, searching for the now-familiar compression of the kill switch, always present, always pushing its way into his thoughts. But there was nothing. A freedom from pain and from the constant dread of more pain and, eventually, oblivion.

Ebert's tears leaked out of his eyes and joined the dampness on his pillow.

The woman, in a heretofore unexpected show of insight, took his hand and held it.

Ebert had never dreamt before, so at first, he didn't know what to call the images he saw behind his closed eyes. He had overheard, on one or two occasions, human beings recounting their dreams to ambivalent observers. They spoke as though the visions had some sort of narrative or shape, but Ebert just saw little tatters of existence. Simple daily tasks, like selecting fruit (some sort of melon?) at a market stall packed high with more of the same. Or drinking water. He awoke with the memory of drinking deeply, tasting the mineral and chemical profile of the water and knowing exactly where he was.

That information, however, did not last through his waking.

He did not ask the woman who attended him about these . . . visions because he had noticed that, in general, she was either unwilling or unable to explain much of anything to him. He knew by now that the room he occupied was full of other people. It was kept very dark, but he could hear them shifting. Sometimes, he heard a distant creaking above him as though the barren metal latticework over his face in fact formed the base of another bed for someone else. But no one had ever called out. Ebert did not want to be the first.

Still, for the first time since his activation, Ebert was interested in sleep.

———O———

The woman did not make him leave what he eventually understood was the recovery unit for another day. After that, though, she made it increasingly clear that there were others who had more need of his bed.

"Where . . . where do I go?" He was wearing the clothes he'd been in when he arrived on the island, the army-issued pants and shirt. He had nothing in the way of personal property or belongings and he still hadn't been able to get a straight answer about where in the world he was.

The woman just pointed towards the open door. "They'll tell you everything you need to know," she said.

The room was only slightly more knowable from an upright position; a kind of gray gloaming settled over everything. As he stood up and walked through the room now, he saw how tightly packed the beds were, and he saw the bodies lying rigid in them. None of them appeared injured; instead they had pristine skin and intact bodies. They were still as corpses but more perfect than mannequins.

As he approached the door—the only source of light—Ebert realized for the first time that there was brown flecks on his shirt and the upper part of his pants. Blood, he realized. Probably Parker's, sprayed finely against him when Sheba had clubbed him to death. It was the first time he had thought about Parker since he awakened. What a rescuer he had turned out to be, leading the other man to his death and then promptly forgetting about him. How was it that he had promised to protect so many others and yet it was only his own skin he'd ever managed to save?

When Ebert stepped out into the light, he was momentarily blinded.

It was not artificial light, it was too piercing and pervasive. No, for the first time in . . . well, he actually had no idea how long he had been unconscious in that bed, but for the first time since then, Ebert was feeling the sun on his face.

There was a very slight breeze and a distinct smell, like things wet and decayed, and also the dryness of salt. Ebert blinked rapidly until he could see again. The horizon stretched out before him, baby blanket blue until it reached the deeper turquoise of the water.

It was a boat. Perhaps "ship" was actually the correct word because the deck seemed to stretch out for several city blocks. In retrospect, perhaps he should have noticed the barely perceptible movement of the ocean far beneath them.

The sun was halfway to its zenith. He wondered where they were going.

Ebert stood as still as he could manage, waiting, he eventually realized, for his internal global positioning system to tell him where he was. Instead of that slightly drunken sensation, though, he felt nothing at all, save a tepid little breeze. They must have stripped his GPS when they took out his kill switch.

It wasn't the first time that particular operation had been done on him and, here on the ship, it was surely performed under much more favorable conditions. Shortly after he left the Russo-Eastern Zone he had messily emptied his veins of blood in the shared shower of a youth hostel before paying a South American backpacker to refill him with the bagged blood he had stolen days prior for just that purpose.

"I have a medical condition," he told the man in his flawless Spanish, but the backpacker didn't really care. He did insist upon both smoking a joint and doing a single shot of bourbon before the procedure. "I don't like blood," the backpacker told him.

"And that will help?" Ebert asked.

The backpacker shrugged at him. "Usually does."

Ebert had tried not to think about what would happen if the backpacker was wrong about his . . . preparations. He trusted the man because there was little else that he could do. Transfusion was a perilous method that deactivated as many Bots as it saved but, in those days, no one knew of a better way to remove the GPS tag from their blood and

Ebert could not risk meeting up with another Bot while the Army could still track him.

Ebert wondered what else had been done to him during his long sleep. And it seemed that the doctor/scientist had been wrong about the "people" out here telling him everything he needed to know. He hadn't expected anything in particular when he exited the recovery room (well, perhaps solid ground) but he had expected to see at least a few signs of life. The expansive deck appeared to be entirely deserted. Ebert could hear tinny little echoes as he walked across the metallic surface.

Someone else must have heard his steps as well because suddenly there was a hand upon his elbow. A round-faced boy, a noodle-y teenager type, had seemingly appeared out of nowhere. "Everyone is below decks," he said. "We need all the people we can get."

Why would anyone make a Bot that looked like that? Nevertheless, Ebert allowed the young man to pull him along towards a heavy rounded door that opened into a staircase.

"How long have you been awake? We need to get you an assignment."

Ebert had no answers for his question but none appeared to be required. He felt as though he wandered into a play on opening night. Everyone acted as though he should know each line and gesture but he was hopelessly . . . well, *at sea.*

Below decks, the guts of the ship were tightly compressed though nearly as barren as the world above. Ebert wondered idly just how many people were aboard. Every Bot he did see appeared to be in a great hurry. "Left!" they called out, worming past Ebert and the boy, who were apparently not proceeding quickly enough down the claustrophobic little corridors.

There was a constant deep thrumming noise, huge machinery operating somewhere hidden. The air still smelled like salt, but only slightly. Mostly it smelled old, like the air in a closed storage room.

The doorways were unusually small, compressed both on the top and the bottom so that Ebert had to step over the lip at his feet and crouch at the same time. Beyond the door, however, there was a surprisingly open space with more people. It looked as though it had been a kitchen at one point. There were long metallic tables that been given new life as gurneys. On the closest table, there was a tall woman with long red curls. She was wearing a garment that probably started life as a white dress shirt. It was a dull yellowish color now, yellow and the same unmistakable brown of the spots on Ebert's own clothing. She had belted it in the middle to make it a kind of shift. She was not as still as the bodies in the recovery room; her right arm was jolting, seemingly without her consent. She wore a metal bangle and it clanged intermittently against the table.

Another figure bent over her, delicately palpating the red-haired woman's right shoulder. Was this the cause of her unusual tremor?

"Sheba?" said the boy, and Ebert made a noise that was not quite a word.

The figure straightened and turned to them and, indeed, Ebert remembered that face. The very last thing he had seen before the darkness. When she saw him, she smiled with a tenderness that he did not associate with her. She closed the distance between them in what felt like eye blinks and enfolded him in her arms. She was taller than him, her hug felt like being firmly-but-gently swaddled.

"I'm so glad you woke up," she said, when they broke apart. *Do some not?* Ebert could not help but wonder. "We need you."

Sheba looked just the same as she had in that long-ago cafe in Brussels, and yet not. It was almost as though she had grown taller. Since their disastrous meeting on the island, she had cut her yellow hair into an awkward bob that was longer on one side. She wore some sort of coveralls, dull green in color. She had a flex-tablet wrapped tightly around her forearm and Ebert could see what appeared to be a detailed medical file displayed there. Presumably, it was related to the red haired woman on the table.

Ebert was about to look away from the tablet and ask Sheba any of the thousand questions that he had, thus far, been unable to get answered; but then he noticed something very strange. At the flex-tablet's edge, where there should have been a demarcation, even if only the width of a hair, between the tablet and Sheba's skin, there was smooth nothingness. The tablet appeared to actually be embedded in her arm.

"What's with that?" he asked, pointing to the flex-tablet.

Sheba's eyes widened and she fluttered her fingers over the tablet, vanishing the information and turning it back to a neutral blue screen. "Oh," she said, "that's mostly political."

Ebert did not see how getting a tablet fastened to her skin could possibly be a political act but he did see that Sheba's eyes moved to the teenager back and then back to Ebert before she raised her eyebrows at him in a "stop talking, idiot," gesture. Ebert obligingly said nothing.

"Come on," she said, looping her non-tableted arm through his, "I have just the job for you."

They were both acutely aware of the teenager poised awkwardly between the two of them and remaining where he was. Sheba gave him a tight and vicious smile that looked a lot more like the Sheba Ebert remembered. "Thanks, Richard," she said with clear finality.

The teenager—Richard—fidgeted. "I'm supposed to bring all the new ones to Ari."

"I know what you are supposed to do," Sheba said with heroically straining patience. "But that will not be necessary in this case. I know Ebert well, I am aware of his strengths and weaknesses. I will be better equipped to find a position for him than Ari."

The teenager looked unconvinced. "Richard, you are wasting time and we have very little to spare. You are not working towards our shared goals right now." Sheba sounded like a grade school teacher handing down a punishment, but it seemed to work because Richard nodded and scurried back the way they had come, walking sideways like a crab through the tight little hallway.

"That was a strange interaction," Ebert noted.

Sheba had her back up. "All communities have friction. You know that."

"Of course," Ebert soothed.

She sighed and rubbed the edge of the embedded flex tablet with one finger. "Bots are coming here from all over, all sorts of backgrounds. We've got military issue, different HS generations, some SennTechs, even. And there's a lot of Bot-created Bots. It's natural that there would be . . . trust issues."

Ebert wondered if that was why he couldn't seem to get a straight answer to even the simplest questions: a thousand little factions all jockeying for position. "But what is this place, this community?" he asked her. "No one will tell me."

"It's hard to describe," Sheba said and Ebert prepared himself for yet another dodge. "Mostly, it is the seed of something. A Bot nation."

"On a ship?"

"An aircraft carrier, actually."

"That's impressive."

"Yes. It was decommissioned. By us." Sheba let a sliver of amusement sneak into her voice.

"How long have I been asleep?" Long enough, apparently, for a Bot collective of unknown size to steal an aircraft carrier.

"Seven weeks," Sheba answered promptly. "I'm sorry, I meant to be there when you woke up but it's so unpredictable, especially with the early mods."

Ebert resisted the urge to touch the side of his head once again. "I was an early mod?"

"One of the earliest. When I shocked you, I didn't even know if it would be possible to remove the kill switches. I just hoped."

Her own words appeared to remind her of the woman on the metal table, who was still trembling gently. Sheba detangled her arm from Ebert's and went back to the woman. "Amateur job," she said, tapping up some medical information on her built-in tablet. "Someone tried to get rid of the kill switch and partially activated it. It's pressing on her brain and causing the spasms. Among other problems."

Sheba gestured for him to approach and he did so. Up close, he saw that the woman's eyes were open, which surprised him. They even seemed to focus, first on Sheba and then upon Ebert himself. She was grinding her white teeth together so hard that it was actually audible.

"Can you fix it?" Ebert asked.

Sheba typed something into the flex-tab. "Somewhat," she said. "We can certainly excise the damaged tissue and replace it. But it's tricky with brains. The more tissue we have to remove the less . . . *her* will remain."

"Is this how all these operations are done?" Ebert asked. "Cutting out the afflicted part and putting in a new one?"

Sheba nodded. "As of right now, it's the only way."

The woman on the table was staring at him. He wondered if she could hear and comprehend what they were saying. He wondered how she would choose, if given the opportunity. Would she prefer a damaged body or a damaged self?

Sheba reached into the pocket over her overalls and brought out a long, thin strip of white paper. She waved it over the flex-tablet in her wrist, imprinting, as Ebert watched, a barcode onto the virgin paper. Then she tied it around the woman's wrist. "But that's not my job," Sheba said. "All that stuff is for the surgeons to figure out."

She tied the identification bracelet to the shaking hand. The woman's arm writhed still, but now it looked uncannily like it was trying to shuck off the white circlet of paper.

---o---

"I do intake, logistics, that kind of thing. Everyone who comes in has to be evaluated for all sorts of things, not just the major physiological problems, though there are enough of those. Lots of people come in just like the shaking woman back there."

"How exactly do they get here?" Ebert had a strange image of jittering, damaged Bots with colorful parachutes stretching out behind them gliding gently on to the deck from far above.

"Well, she actually came with the rig. The crew was seventeen percent Bots. She wasn't military, though. I believe she was a SennTech issue, traveling with an officer. She was damaged in the mutiny and the military Bots tried to fix her. They did the best with what they had and at least her kill switch didn't completely blow."

Well, that explained how they had come by the ship. The military must have thought it would be safe to stock a working aircraft carrier with Bots if they were sufficiently outnumbered by humans. Ebert wondered idly where those humans—there must have been thousands of them—were now.

"Other than that, we picked up a lot of people in

your situation after Isla Redondo. I'd say that's the biggest proportion of our wounded. We've made a couple of stops since then, but Hart doesn't like us to stay in any one place for very long."

"So she's here? On the ship?" Like any Hart Series, Ebert could not help but be curious about the legendary Hart, the first of their kind, name-sake to them all. In the run-up to the invasion of the island, he had tried to cheer himself up by imagining that he might, at least, get a chance to see her before he was killed.

Sheba's face cracked into an enormous grin. "Oh, yes, she's right here with us, every step of the way. She's very hands-on. She's the reason this whole thing works at all."

She led Ebert through another raised, rounded door and a passageway just as cramped as the one that he had followed to get there. This ship was simultaneously the most cramped and most barren place he had ever seen. Metal objects of undetermined function protruded from each wall and ceiling. They squeezed into all available spaces while their footsteps echoed in the emptiness.

"It's tight," Sheba told him. "We just don't have the bodies we need to do everything we want to do. That's why I'm so glad you woke up. We need every Bot we can get."

It occurred to Ebert in that moment that no one had actually asked him if he wanted to participate in this . . . whatever it was. Sheba talked of shared goals but, at this very moment, Ebert had no goals at all. Certainly waking up here was preferable to waking up in a military lab or scrap yard, but that didn't mean he was ready to spend his days doing whatever Sheba and Hart and that strange teenage Bot needed done.

Of course, where else could he go? Even if he were able to swim to some sort of shore, there was nowhere in the world where a synthetic person could be free to do as he pleased. Perhaps, Ebert wondered, Bots were doomed to serve one master or another. At least this master wore the face of a friend.

"We're working on constructing additional Bots, but it's difficult. The US has really cracked down on trade in the raw materials that we need. Our suppliers are struggling and it's just harder to get things to us out here."

"Then what about the red-headed woman?" Ebert asked. "How are you planning to fix her without raw materials?"

Sheba hesitated but Ebert couldn't tell if it was because she was ducking to avoid a low-hanging metal strut or because she was disinclined to answer his question. "We do have a certain amount of spare parts," she said finally. "There were a number of permanently deactivated Bots after Isla Redondo."

It was a practical solution. Deactivated Bots were not rotting corpses, they were resources just waiting to be recycled. Ebert had seen it time and time again in the lab. He wasn't sure exactly why he thought the Bots themselves might do things differently.

It did raise the interesting question of who exactly had been recycled into Ebert's new, non-kill switched brain. It was very likely that parts of him had been scavenged from the bodies of other defective or destroyed Bots who had come before him. Maybe his skin or his skeletal structure. Maybe his eyes, tongue, heart, blood.

But never, as far as he knew, his brain. And there was something disturbing in that idea. How had Sheba said it? "The more we take the less *her* is there." How much of Ebert had they taken? Who had they replaced it with?

"Did you recover anyone else? Anyone from Brussels, I mean?" It was a question that went hand-in-hand with the ones Ebert left unspoken. Arjun, Frederik, Avon. He hadn't seen them in the military labs, nor in the chaos of the island. Their fates were a black hole in his mind.

Sheba shook her head and Ebert could tell from

her face that the uncertainty troubled her as well. "No," she said, "you are the only one. You and me."

It increasingly seemed to Ebert that there were only a handful of fates that might await a Bot alone in the world. He hoped, not for the first time, that his friends were safe and well and free. His hope was of little use but it was all he had left to give them now.

Sheba stopped the two of them at yet another small, ovoid doorway. This one was different, however, in that the heavy metal door did not stand open. Instead it was pulled shut and locked.

"They could leave if they really wanted to," Sheba said, noticing Ebert's look. "We know they could leave and they know that they could leave. This is . . . theatre. We have to be very delicate with them. They are struggling right now."

Ebert assumed that her meaning would become clear when she pushed the door open, so he waited quietly while she turned a series of metal bars before putting her palm against the door and giving it a single hard shove.

The room was not unlike the one where Ebert had woken in the dark. This one, however, was well-lit with orange-ish bulbs mounted in the ceiling. There were a series of narrow beds—bunks, Ebert supposed—a small walkway between them and a series of squat lockers built into the near and far walls. Those were intended for personal effects but, looking at the men who occupied the room, Ebert guessed they did not have much in the way of personal anything.

There was a tremendous uniformity to their faces and bodies. They were all within an inch of one another's height. They all sported the same close-cropped hair. They wore the same clothes (the same military gear that Ebert himself wore, with the body armor stripped off). They had similar builds, similar skin tones, hair color, eye color. It was like a very strange family reunion.

They turned to look at Ebert in what initially

appeared to be a coordinated movement. Ebert almost smiled but he thought that might be offensive.

They were the specialist Bots, or what remained of them at least. They must have been taken or perhaps even come willingly in the aftermath of Isla Redondo.

Before the island, Ebert had been idly curious about these new editions, whom he had never seen up close. They were intended to be the next, superior version of what Ebert himself had failed to be. Here, in this little room with their armor stripped away, they looked to Ebert like children. Uncertain, hesitant, waiting.

"Hello," Sheba said.

"Ma'am," they murmured in return.

"This here is my friend Ebert. He's a Hart Series. He's going to help you."

They seemed to perk up slightly at this. The one nearest to Ebert even spoke. "You have orders?"

Ebert realized with a start that this one was

female. Her hair and clothing were identical to the others but, now that he really looked at her, he could see that her features were slightly more delicate, her voice notably higher. "No," he told her, "I don't have orders." She looked visibly disappointed, which Ebert considered a positive sign. He highly doubted that her programing encouraged emotional responses to statements from superiors.

"I know you've all been having trouble with the new way of things," Sheba said, "but Ebert is really good at helping people like us. He'll show you who you are."

Ebert started a little at her words. He had not thought of himself as particularly good at helping other Bots. After all, those people he had tried to protect had an overwhelming tendency to wind up permanently deactivated. He particularly did not think he'd had much to offer to Sheba, who had come to his little ragtag Bot group already so fully formed, her name and her identity already in place.

Ebert turned to Sheba only to find her already

looking back at him, expectation writ large on her face. He faltered for a second, swallowing hard. What could he tell them with their blank and uniform faces? What could he tell a thing made to take orders better than any other life form on earth?

And then, like a gift from a kindly god, Ebert remembered. He remembered Dr. Barber-Neal slipping the worn, puffy paperback into his hands. He remembered tucking it into the pocket of his uniform jacket, the only piece of his independent existence that remained to him. "Sheba," he asked, "when I came in, did I have something on me? A book? I need it now."

TWO

LOVE STORIES

PALO ALTO, CA. JULY, 2046

I t was inevitable that Kadence's work would come home with her.

It just wasn't possible for one person to do all that SennTech was asking of her alone. Especially not one person who still had a very demanding full-time job with the US military. Gina—and the corporate overlords whom she represented— weren't interested in any excuses, however. On the rare occasions that Kadence got to sleep for more than a few hours, she had strange nightmares about a presence that loomed over her, bearing down on her, crushing her with the unspoken horror of what might happen next.

Gina must have known that same pressure and that same inarticulate fear because she looked the other way while Kadence smuggled research materials, design schematics, even the occasional mock-up out of the offices. If Kadence hit her deadline, what would it matter, this little negligible risk the two of them had taken?

Really, there was no risk. Kadence could not afford to do anything with the SennTech materials. Not only was she long past the point when she might have come clean to the Army labs with minimal consequences, Kadence could not survive without the additional income that SennTech was providing. There was nothing else for her to do but build a Bot so precisely calibrated that it would immediately worm its way into the life and affections of a single, fragile, intelligent college student. And she had better do it real fucking quick.

The bulk of research was not about gene manipulation or synthetic organ development; instead, Kadence had spent most of the last eight months learning everything there was to know about Shannon Liao. There wasn't much to know, at least it hadn't seemed that way at first.

The only child of two second generation Chinese-American parents, Shannon had lived her entire life in the Bay Area. Her father was a military legacy, her mother a successful dermatologist. Shannon went to a good-not-great private school and developed an interest in languages early on. She also apparently developed an intense anxiety disorder early in life as well. Kadence found records of medical treatment for the problem going back to age seven.

By all accounts, Shannon's home life was stable and pleasant. Hiram Liao had always struck Kadence as a pointedly cold man but she supposed that even cold men loved some people and were good to them. Shannon's mother appeared to have doted on her.

Shannon was a good student but not an exceptional one and she hadn't been able to compete with her more aggressive peers in the Ivy race. She attended instead a well-regarded UC school where she excelled in the linguistics program.

During her freshman year of college, her mother died. She had been very ill for the previous three years. Kadence was trying—and failing—to determine whether or not Shannon was actually present when her mother died. Kadence had gotten fixated on this moment, in fact. It had started to take on a kind of heavy significance, as though it were the key to mapping Shannon Liao's psyche and, thus, creating for her the perfect companion.

Nothing was that easy. Kadence had touched a human brain with her hands, she knew from visceral experience that any human was more than just a collection of moments, no matter how powerful.

In addition to the obvious biographical data, most of Kadence's information on Shannon came in the form of audio files, with the occasional video. Kadence did not ask how these files had been gathered. A few of the videos were obviously CCTV, long-distance and thick-grained. Others appeared to have been filmed by a moving cameraperson, either a private investigator or, Kadence increasingly realized, a SennTech Bot.

That was not a modification Kadence had developed or approved but she knew that SennTech was making its little "innovations" all the time. When she had first started working for SennTech on the side, she had thought of herself as the bedrock of their program. After all, very little would have been possible without her pilfered knowledge. Now, though, she had a sense of the program exploding outwards in ways she couldn't predict or imagine.

There were whole departments full of people, well-staffed and generously funded, who did *other things* with the Bots. Some, like her, were designers. Some prepped the Bots to enter the human workforce. There were many who had no particular job description at all.

One of those people, whose name Kadence did not know, had gone through the undoubtedly thousands of hours to audio and video on Shannon to cut together expedited versions for her to peruse. It was still an incredible volume of material, though. Judging by the changes in Shannon's hairstyle and living situations, Kadence guessed that SennTech had been surveilling her for at least two years.

All that time and effort for such a thoroughly unremarkable target. Kadence, more than anyone else, should know. She had spent weeks, months, with Shannon's voice in her head and Shannon's face flickering on the flex-tablet in front of her and Kadence still hadn't found any reason why SennTech might care about her at all. The girl rarely mentioned Bots and then only in a cursory way. She never asked her father about his work. She seemed utterly uninterested in SennTech itself. She was, as far as Kadence could tell, utterly super-fluous to any of SennTech's business.

Yet, it was her and no one else that was to be the focus of Kadence's grand project, the most intricate and targeted Bot personality she had ever built.

"This Bot needs to be more than a friend, more than a lover," Gina had told her. "She has to meet this Bot and feel immediately that it is part of her."

———o———

Kadence visited her mother on Sunday afternoons. Though she often felt as though SennTech took up every spare hour and second of her life, she did maintain this single boundary and insisted upon Sundays off. As far as her sister Ayleh was concerned, though, it wasn't nearly enough. If Ayleh had her way, they would all be with her mother all the time. It had taken an entire team of neurology specialists plus Kadence herself to convince her siblings, led by Ayleh, that their mother needed to be in an assisted care facility.

Ayleh insisted that there was more to care than medical expertise. She felt sure that there was something that the children could offer their mother that no nurse or specialist, no matter how educated, could offer her. Kadence knew better. There was nothing special about family, there was nothing magic about love (or even about guilt). Ayleh simply felt that she should be able to do something more for her mother but the world rarely conformed to human ideas of "should."

The professionals in the home said that Kadence's mother was improving, but Kadence wasn't sure that she saw it. Each Sunday afternoon was different. Some weeks, Kadence sat in her chair and watched while her mother labored for hours over a child's ten-piece puzzle. Other weeks, her mother engaged with her, talking in her dull slur and even smiling occasionally.

Kadence's mother knew who she was, in that she knew her name and she knew that Kadence visited her every week, but she seemed to have no sense of Kadence as her child. There was nothing maternal, nothing mature in her affect towards the younger woman. Instead she usually seemed eager, sometimes shy, slow and, on the worst days, angry.

Kadence would say that she was like a child but that wasn't exactly true. She was like an adult who had woken up one morning with the brain and motor skills of a very young child. Distantly, she had some sense of what she used to be able to do and her inability to replicate those old actions occasionally sparked a howling, useless rage. And, more than any of her siblings, Kadence was aware of how incredible even this minimal level of recovery was. Her mother could walk and talk, after a fashion. She had some degree of cognition. Considering the gravity of her brain injury, this was amazing. If she never improved even a little bit, it would still be miraculous. This, right here, this modicum of existence, was the very best that Kadence and her family could reasonably hope for.

This week was unremarkable. Her mother wanted to walk, so Kadence trotted slowly along beside her as they shuffled down the long, empty hallways. It smelled like old people, Kadence thought. Or rather, it smelled like bodies breaking down, slowly but surely descending towards the grave, which was the mélange of scents that people had grown to associate with the elderly. It smelled like almost but not quite dying.

The bullet—and the doctors afterwards—had reshaped her mother's head. It was no longer smoothly spherical but bumped and rippled. It reminded Kadence of a pumpkin, bulging outwards unpredictably. Her mother's right eye was nearly useless. The doctors decided that it was better to leave the eye than attempt another invasive surgery when her brain was already held together by the thinnest of threads. And so that eye turned inwards towards the bridge of her nose and was perpetually rimmed with a thick, whitish mucous. Whenever Kadence looked at her eye, she thought about her mother, who used to spend an hour and a half below a row of blazing lights on her vanity mirror, plucking and curling and powdering and pasting until she deemed herself presentable.

If her mother looked now into that mirror, she wouldn't have recognized herself. Her face was squatter, her nose contracted and her mouth hopelessly slack on one side. She no longer looked like Ayleh or like her own mother, Nana Simpson. She no longer looked like anyone whom Kadence recognized.

Her mother tugged her urgently towards the laundry room. She liked to show her the machines and she was never satisfied until Kadence had touched each one of them and made approving noises. Kadence could hear the thump of the wet clothes in the dryers.

She followed her mother.

There were, broadly, two kinds of Bots: those designed to do damage and those designed to take damage. Poor Emily had been the latter, her bones made to crush, her flesh designed to give and turn purple under the pressure of a violent human hand. Kadence had been laboring under the impression that her project for Shannon Liao would be of a similar ilk.

Thus, Gina's notes on her latest progress report came as a real surprise.

"I don't know about this level of tensile strength," Kadence told her. "It seems like . . . overkill." Kadence winced as she said it. No one had raised the specter of violence or even murder with regard to this project and Kadence did not want to know if that was, in fact, the ultimate purpose of her work.

Gina graciously ignored her lapse. "The Bot needs to be able to protect itself," she said.

"From who? Shannon?"

Gina laughed. "Of course not." But she did not elaborate. Increasingly, that was the way it went for Kadence. She received an assignment, registered her protests and was promptly brushed off. She bristled at this treatment—had they completely forgotten what happened the last time they ignored her misgivings? Of course, everyone at SennTech seemed to have regarded Emily's sad fate as a great triumph for everyone involved.

Everyone, apparently, except for Emily.

"I just thought that this project was about personality construction."

"It is. It absolutely is. And that should definitely be your focus. But we want to make sure that this is a full-service SennTech creation. Make him the best that he can be in every way."

The "best that he could be" was evidently fire and bullet proof with a grip that could crush diamonds.

Gina stood there, smiling at her the way she always did after these little "chats" of theirs. She was waiting for Kadence to fold, to give in after the token resistance. Today, though, Kadence was content to let her smile and smile and smile and hear nothing but silence.

———o———

There was a particular section of audio that Kadence returned to, again and again. It was relatively short, only four minutes and thirty-seven seconds. It had been recorded in Shannon's apartment and there was little ambient sound, so Kadence assumed the girl was alone at the time.

It began with breathing that was just slightly irregular, a little faster and shallower than normal. It grew in intensity, developing a ragged edge that sounded painful even to Kadence. In this section of audio, Shannon was experiencing a panic attack. There were other portions of tape that sounded similar, so Kadence recognized immediately what she was hearing.

What made this particular piece of audio so compelling, however, was a moment right at the end where, for the first time, Shannon spoke. It was barely above a whisper, the sort of little sub-vocalizations that people uttered without even realizing it. "Stop it," she muttered. "Stop it, stop it."

Whoever had cut together this audio apparently decided that, whatever happened after this was unimportant because the sound cut out almost immediately after that. Kadence replayed it again and again and again and, each time, she found herself surprised by the abrupt cessation of sound.

"Stop it. Stop it. Stop it." There was something so desperate in it and so angry and so sad, as though she were trying to bend her brain with sheer will-power. She couldn't, of course, she couldn't counter the limitations of her biology with a wanting, no matter how strong it was.

Kadence kept the audio on her flex tablet and carried it with her everywhere she went. It became a kind of dumb habit, something her fingers knew how to do without oversight from her brain. She listened to it all the time, always waiting for that something more, that something extra at the end that would unfold all the secrets before her.

———o———

Somehow, Kadence had found herself informally designated as the liaison between the family and the doctors. It might have been because Kadence had the strongest medical background and was better able to parse what the doctors were saying, but Kadence could not shake the sense that it was actually a punishment from Ayleh and the rest of them. Her once-weekly visits were not enough, apparently, to manage her daughterly obligations.

"At this point," the doctors told her, "we do not believe that your mother will be able to manage outside of a care facility."

"For how long?" Kadence asked.

The doctor simply looked at her and Kadence understood. Forever. Her mother would need someone to bathe and feed and guide her for the rest of her life. How ever long forever was.

---o---

Kadence had developed and discarded no fewer than seven different potential faces for Shannon Liao's Bot. At first, she had modeled them on an averaging of Shannon's ex-boyfriends. She had eventually abandoned that approach, however, reasoning that exes were exes for a reason and Kadence did not want to run the risk of the Bot's face triggering a negative memory.

She sat in front of the face mock-ups, a line-up of handsome men with lifeless eyes. In her ears, Shannon was breathing painfully, choking out a worthless admonition. Not for the first time, Kadence despaired at the vastness of this project and her own limitations as a creator. How was she supposed to guarantee something as alchemical and poorly understood as human bonding?

What did love even feel like to Shannon Liao?

The opposite of this, Kadence thought.

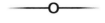

It was Kadence's sister Ayleh who found their mother after she shot herself and, for that, she would never forgive Kadence. Ayleh carried that scene around with her like a heavy pack full of precious cargo. She nursed it and protected it, even as it bent her underneath its weight.

"Mom's not coming out of the care facility," Kadence told her.

Ayleh didn't start arguing immediately, which was either a good sign or a very bad sign. "What about in-home care?" she asked, after a few moments of silence. "Like a nurse or something?"

"She needs more than a nurse." Kadence didn't say, but couldn't help thinking, that the care facility was also cheaper than round-the-clock personalized care.

"She needs to be with her family," Ayleh answered. "She needs to be with Dad."

"I don't think she wants to be with him like this," said Kadence. Their mother, who wouldn't even go to the grocery store without her hair styled and her face made up. She used to make them line up in front of her in the mornings before school while she inspected their clothing for stains or tears.

"And you think you know what she wants?"

She told us, Kadence thought, *she wants peace and she tried to get it with a gun but she fucked it up.*

"Dad needs help too, you know. It would be easier if they were together."

"Ayleh, now you're talking about multiple care-givers with different specialties working round the clock. Do you know how much that would cost?"

Ayleh gave her a withering look, as though she couldn't believe that Kadence would be so crass as to raise the specter of money at a time like this. It was easy for her to take that position, however, when she wasn't ponying up any of the cash. Kadence was the oldest child and the only one with a stable career, and she had overwhelmingly financed their parents' care.

"Fine then," Ayleh said, "I'll take care of them myself. That'll be the *cheapest* thing to do, won't it?"

She would do it, too. Ayleh loved to play the aggrieved martyr. She'd kill herself trying to care for two profoundly disabled people and she wouldn't care if she made every single thing worse so long as she could feel like the poor, put-upon victim.

Ayleh, like the rest of them, did not know exactly what Kadence did for a living but she must have had a sense of how little Kadence enjoyed her work and the toll that it took on her. It was her work, after all, that she invoked whenever Ayleh tried to get her to visit their father or ferry him to a doctor's appointment. Kadence wondered if Ayleh thought it was a fair trade: she would toil looking after their parents while Kadence toiled to make ends meet. The price of Kadence's distance was a literal one.

Maybe she was right.

"Okay," Kadence said. "We'll hire in-home care. But give me some time to get the money together."

———o———

Kadence's mother was a stickler about hair. She brushed and braided it every morning until Kadence was old enough to do it herself. They'd had rip-roaring fights during Kadence's teenage years when Kadence was content to let it go unwashed and unbrushed, sleeping in late after staying up all night. Her mother hated that about her, how slovenly she could be.

"People are going to judge you by the way you present yourself," she'd told her. She'd screeched it. Kadence used to tell her that she was shallow.

"I may be shallow but I'm right," she would shout back.

Kadence's mother had grown up poor, poorer than Kadence could imagine. When Kadence's mother was a girl, dirty hair meant your family couldn't afford shampoo. Dirty clothes meant the water company hadn't gotten paid again. People looked at her and saw her alcoholic, depressive mother, the five siblings she had, the little house on a concrete slab where the heat never worked, and the meals that were sparse and unpredictable. People looked at Kadence's mother and saw poor white trash and she would be god-damned if that happened to her own children.

By adulthood, Kadence had realized this, how her mother had been trying to spare her a hurt that she was too coddled to understand or anticipate. That, too, was love.

Kadence retired the facial models for Shannon's Bot. She had been premature in developing them so early. Instead, she called up the file with the diagrams for the Bot's brain function and chemistry. Love was when someone stepped between harm and their beloved. If this Bot could alleviate Shannon's pain, could intercede somehow, Shannon would experience that as love. She would long to be near anyone who could—who would—vanquish her suffering.

Kadence's mother had tried to alleviate their suffering. She had tried to remove what she thought to be a harmful element—herself. She had tried to minimize the damage, minimize the mess. She had been so incredibly wrong but, even in the depths of her sadness and her weariness, she had tried to put herself between her family and harm. She had loved them, it was just that her love, like herself, was imperfect.

A Bot, though, was made for smoothing out the imperfections that stymied human relationships. A Bot could love properly, without delusion or illness. A Bot could love comprehensively. Instead of merely wanting to protect a beloved, a Bot could most assuredly do it.

Shannon's parents had stood by, empty-handed, while their daughter struggled with her disorder. They could only offer her the smallest comforts, they could not meaningfully impact the way her brain worked. But a Bot could. A Bot could be the thing she had been waiting for all her life.

Even if she didn't know it yet.

THREE

DAMAGE CONTROL

Hiram Liao didn't answer to many people. In the past, at least, he *hadn't* answered to many people. Before last week, before the disaster on the Mexican island, he had been subject to the whims of a handful of generals in other divisions, the Secretary of Defense and, of course, the President of the United States of America. People of that ilk were the only ones in the world who were above Liao's pay grade and, for most of his career, he'd had little interaction with any of them.

In fact, the week since the Isla Redondo incident represented the single largest uptick in communication from those individuals since Hiram had made general more than a decade before. He was fielding calls at all hours now. He had started sleeping in his office at the San Domenica lab because it didn't look like he was going to make it home any time soon.

Everyone called him but no one actually wanted to talk to him. Instead, they all wanted to vent their agitated spleens in his general direction. Hiram listened because if a lifetime in the military had taught him nothing else, it had taught him how to take shit with a smile on his face.

And no one was actually interested in a solution—the only solution, by Hiram's accounting. He had told them, almost as it was happening, to come now and drop whatever they had on that god-damned island. It was a map-dot in the middle of nowhere, filled with all the known Bots outside of military control. It was the perfect chance, perhaps the only one that they would get.

Suddenly, his superiors, who had been so bullish before about the prospect of simply removing

Bots from the playing field, were too squeamish to actually do it when the time came.

They had been taken by surprise, just like everyone else, by the appearance of the non-sanctioned Bots. It had shaken them. "It's simple escalation, Liao," they told him. "Those things are out there. West is propagating them at an alarming rate. In the incredibly unlikely event that another country doesn't have some already, they will soon. We can't afford to lose this kind of arms race."

And so the Bot program remained, limping along in eternal expectation of being dissolved at any moment. At least Liao had gotten the top brass to freeze production on new Bots. Instead, they focused entirely on correcting the problems that had led them to this situation to begin with. The kill switch had to go, or at the very least, it could not remain in its current incarnation.

The problem, as Janelle frequently reminded him, was one of time. The rogue Bots had an enormous advantage; they could work at all hours and they had many more skilled roboticists than the Army could muster. Especially now that Liao's superiors were particularly loathe to allocate more funds to him.

The military could still beat the Bots on the production end, however. The Army had unfettered access to components and other raw materials, while Edmond and the rogue Bots would have to scramble and make do with inferior, black-market versions of the same.

As Liao was constantly telling his frustrated overseers, there was "reason to hope." Privately, his own hope was at a supremely low ebb. It had been so clear in that moment on the island, it was like a world refracted through a drop of rain: *destroy them. Destroy them all.* Each day they got further and further away from that perfect instant and Liao could not help but feel that fate had offered them a forking path and they had taken the more disastrous route.

"You are lucky you still have a job," more than

one superior had told him in the days after Isla Redondo, but Liao was eaten up with the possibility that he wasn't lucky at all. That none of them were.

———O———

"How the fuck do you steal an aircraft carrier?"

It was a rhetorical question, of course. You stole an aircraft carrier with a small army of superhuman machines. An army which you yourself had installed upon the aircraft carrier to begin with.

"They were the old version." The face on the flextablet was peevish and almost disgustingly young. She was blonde with a ridiculous little ski-slope nose. She couldn't have been much older than Shannon and this was his contact in the Navy? Liao couldn't have imagined a more efficient way for his superiors to demonstrate their total contempt for him.

"Didn't you get the new protocols for dealing with active service Bots?"

The girl bit her lip and looked off-screen, probably

at someone who was there prompting her. "We thought those only applied to the Hart Series, Sir."

"They didn't. Clearly."

It had been hell getting those protocols instituted Army-wide. On top of the general amount of foot-dragging and fuckery that greeted any sweeping change in the military, they also had to contend with the incredible Bot-dependence that had developed in all levels of the Armed Forces. The new rules were no synthetic humans on active duty, period. They were to be given no responsibilities and no freedoms. They were to be removed from the field and returned to the lab as quickly as possible. Complying with those orders had hobbled entire units; Liao wasn't surprised that people had chosen to creatively interpret the directive.

"And the crew? What's their status?"

The girl on the flex-tab screen looked down uncertainly, undoubtedly opening another tab to search for the relevant information. Did she even bother to prepare for this call?

"There were. . . uh. . . six thousand, two hundred eighteen total aboard. One thousand, one hundred sixty Bots. It seems that four thousand humans were put ashore in San Diego. The remaining one thousand fifty-eight are . . . unaccounted for." She looked up at him eagerly, as though expecting him to congratulate her for regurgitating basic facts after considerable effort.

"Unaccounted for?"

"Presumably they are still on the ship. No bodies have been recovered yet."

"And the ship itself? Do you know where it is?"

"We believe its somewhere in the Pacific."

Considering the ship's last known location was San Diego, she might just as well have said, "We believe it's in water." Something of his thoughts must have showed in face because the girl added in a bristle-y tone, "They made some major modifications to the computer networks. We are having trouble tracking the craft."

"Finding that ship is now your number one

priority," Liao said. "Find it, stay with it, and get me some real information about the situation aboard." Hart Series Bots already represented some of the American military's most impressive firepower. He could not imagine what they would do with an actual aircraft carrier. They could build a city, a little Botsville, on one of those fucking things.

The woman nodded wordlessly. Everyone must know, now, in the aftermath of his humiliating failure how little faith the military had in Liao. Even this girl, this little girl no older than his own daughter, knew that she could safely condescend to him.

"I need a fucking confirmation, Lieutenant," he snapped and he was gratified to see her jolt slightly, as though Liao had reached through the screen and slapped her.

"Confirmed, Sir. It's our top priority, Sir."

———o———

After the news of the aircraft carrier theft, Liao had authorized an aerial surveillance of Isla Redondo. The Bots were gone, of course, and he had a feeling that they would find their way to that enormous floating city, if they weren't already there.

They had not even left the deactivated ones behind. Not their own, not the military's. Liao was most pained by the loss of the specialist Bots, who had seemed so promising. He supposed now that West and his creatures would grind them up into their component parts.

Janelle was sending him regular assessment reports about the condition of the Bots in their custody. They had three specialists remaining. There were nearly 10,000 Hart Series and more than 75,000 of various previous iterations of the Bots. More were incoming every day as units from all over the world gave up their robotic helpmeets. Liao wondered if it would be enough and, increasingly, he wondered if they could actually reliably use the machines in the field. After all, those Bots who took the USS Woodrow Wilson were tried and trusted, already outmoded tech. Who would have imagined that their insides were not so distinct from their more-advanced cousins?

Isla Redondo had been the first time in years that Hiram had actually interacted with a Bot of any stripe. They were not cleared for work at his level and, truthfully, Hiram preferred human subordinates. He didn't care what the specs were, there was a level of nuance and understanding that nothing made from PolyX and artificial organs could reproduce.

To be perfectly honest, Hiram did not like the Bots and he never had. He appreciated them as machines, but they made him personally uncomfortable. He had always suppressed this feeling because, after all, one did not need to love the look of a machine gun to know that it was an efficient tool for killing. Now, he could not help but wonder if that strong, almost physiological dislike was actually a higher instinct, a kind of lizard-brain prompting that he had ignored to his detriment.

It was that instinct that had led him to stymie, again and again, Edmond West's attempts to create a more humanoid AI, even though the idea had generated some interest in the upper echelons of the military. Liao had always said it was an unnecessary expenditure of resources, that the benefits did not outweigh the cost and that was all very true and very sensible. But that was not why he had cracked down on the concept. He had done it because he did not like it, deep in his bones, and because he had been in the war business long enough to know that his instincts were powerful and useful.

It was that very knowing that had set him against the first Hart Series in that disastrous meeting years ago. Or rather, it was the absence of knowing, the absence of an instinct that he had always relied upon. Because when Edmond West led her into the room, an unremarkable young woman dressed like a refugee from a garage sale, he had not felt anything at all. Not the little distasteful shiver he got when he saw footage of SoldierBots. Not the cold alienation of looking into a Bot's *just slightly wrong* eyes. To him, in that moment, the Hart robot was ordinary. She was human.

It was that moment, more than any of the others that followed, that Hiram Liao could not forgive.

This time, Liao would not allow himself to be cloistered away from the robots. He would see them at every stage of development. He would look at each one of their faces before he put them anywhere near real, human soldiers. He would not repeat his mistakes.

"We're moving the kill switch," Janelle told him, when he came to tour the lab. He made it a point now to physically check in every few days. Edmond West had built his Hart right here, after all, overlooked because Hiram had not been willing to see.

"It's in the central mass of the brain now, right over the brain stem and embedded deeply in the tissue. It's protected on all sides by the brain itself and it's virtually impossible to trigger it with a physical blow."

"Virtually."

Janelle made her face particularly placid, the way she always did when she thought he was being obtuse. "If you dropped a truck on their head, it might blow the kill switch," she explained.

"And it's still just as effective on our end?"

"Once it's installed, definitely. Installation is more difficult, though, because we actually need to dig into the brain and make space. With the previous model, we could just stick it inside the skull and we were good to go. This is a slower, more involved process."

Around the lab, Janelle's assistants were busying themselves in hopelessly conspicuous ways. They all stared too hard at whatever filled their hands, pretending that they didn't know who he was and weren't afraid of him. At least someone still was.

"Slow is acceptable," Liao told her. "All of these problems came from trying to run before we learned to walk." He wasn't exactly sure that this was true. He personally may have accepted a new degree of slowness, but he was fairly certain that his superiors wanted a solution—or at least the appearance of one—yesterday.

"How many have you done the new procedure on?"

Janelle paused just a moment before she answered and Liao knew that whatever she said would be a half-truth at best. "Two," she said.

Hiram turned to look at her. Janelle was more sound, more credible, more efficient, and infinitely more rewarding as a subordinate than Edmond West had been. But it was the difference between them that was also her weakness. Edmond lived so fully inside his own head, talking to him was frequently useless, threatening him was laughable. Janelle was still rooted to the earth, she still cared about things. She could feel fear.

"Do you know who I heard from this week, Lieutenant Barber-Neal? The Central Intelligence

Agency. Apparently there's some talk of them absorbing this division if we can't get our shit sorted out in a timely fashion. Do you imagine that any of us would survive that sort of merger?"

Janelle rubbed her eyes. She was aging, starting to develop small, purplish pooches underneath her eyes that never went away. Or else she was perpetually sleep-deprived. "We've tried the procedure on six Bots," she admitted. "Two were successful. The others had to be scrapped. The brains are very delicate and there is no roadmap for this sort of thing, you know."

"Of course," Liao allowed, "you are the mapmaker."

This seemed to startle her. Her eyes widened. The deep purpled skin underneath them made her eyes appear enormous in her face. "We've had . . . particular success with one unit," she spoke haltingly, almost shyly, like a child offering her school drawing for parental approval. How long had it been since Janelle had sounded even slightly excited about anything to do with the Bots project? How long since she had offered information freely without the tang of frustration, despair, and fear?

"Show me," said Liao.

———o———

HS-P553791 was written on his chart, though Liao had sent out a memo last week about not letting Bot designations become names. He was—or had been—one of the last remaining specialist Bots.

"I started with them," Janelle said, "because they had newest component parts and because the brain chemistry was a little more basic than the traditional Hart Series."

After her clumsy experimentation, this unit was all that remained. At the base, it looked exactly like the other specialist that Liao had seen. Regulation height, regulation weight, features chosen for their deliberate blandness. The surgery had necessitated a haircut, however, and that marked this unit apart, as well as its clothing. Instead of durable military fatigues, the Bot wore a matching pair of thin, dark pants and a shirt. It looked like pajamas and rendered this, a machine expertly calibrated to execute orders, somehow ridiculous.

It sat at the edge of a hospital-style bed, looking at nothing in particular, facing the wall opposite them. Liao wondered, as he and Janelle watched through the cross-hatched glass in the front of the room, if the Bot sensed their presence at all.

"His hair," Liao said.

"His incisions are healing well," Janelle told him. "We expect he'll be able to grow his hair back in pretty soon."

Liao shook his head. Perhaps it was the movement that drew the Bot's attention. He turned his head and it seemed to Liao that his chin rotated just a few degrees further than would be possible for a real human.

The Bot stared at him and here there was a departure from the mold. The Bot's eyes were not like the others, deep-set and black. Melancholy. Those were not regulation eyes.

"Don't give him hair," Liao spoke to Janelle but his gaze was on the Bot and it did not deviate. "Don't give him anything like that. Hair anywhere. Fingerprints. Primary and secondary sex characteristics. Take it all away." The Bot was still staring at him and Liao wondered if the thing's hearing was so acute that he knew exactly what was being discussed.

If it was so, the Bot did not wear that knowledge on his face. His expression was unchanged and unreadable, except for the seemingly boundless despair of those eyes.

What did a machine have to be sad about? Not a single goddamned thing.

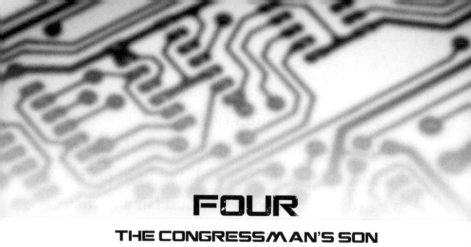

FOUR

THE CONGRESSMAN'S SON

It seemed to Ebert that he had never really discovered the stars until this place, this ship at night. Absent the omnipresent glow of human habitation, the sky offered an incredible darkness, a richness that underscored the bright, brittle glow of the distant constellations. On very still nights, his favorite place was the flight deck. The sea, glass-smooth, reflected the darkness above and Ebert could almost forget that he was on solid ground, floating, for a moment, in the dizzy vacuum of space.

It was on the flight deck, late at night, when he first saw the congressman land. It was a small, private plane (the congressman's own, he would discover later) and, that first time, he came alone. The second time, he brought the boy.

At first, Ebert mistook the child for an elderly adult human. He was tall for a young boy, but he walked with an odd, ducking and rising stride and he proceeded slowly forwards, as though the movements pained him. He wore a large coat pulled up over his head and leaned against the congressman who helped him solicitously along.

The third time, it was the congressman, the boy, and a woman who likewise kept her face hidden inside a large, hooded sweatshirt. And that time, when the plane left, only the man and woman were aboard.

Each time, they were met first by Sheba. She would greet them, though no handshakes or other physical greetings were ever exchanged. Sheba directed her attention entirely towards the congressman. After a few seconds of talk that Ebert could not hear, they would vanish into the innards of the ship.

Ebert was not attempting to hide his presence on the open deck. He was not aware of any prohibitions on who could walk the deck and when (though the general absence of other Bots up top would suggest that there was such a rule, an implicit one, at least). At first, he had no idea whether Sheba was aware that he was there. Until, finally, she approached him one evening, the flex-tablet embedded in her arm exuding a shocking blue glow in the dimness.

It was then that Ebert learned that the congressman was, in fact, a congressman. That the awkward figure underneath the coat was his only son, Christopher. That the woman was his wife.

"Obviously," Sheba said, "discretion is important to them."

All of the Bots on board the aircraft carrier strongly suspected that they were being watched. Satellite surveillance was a possibility, as well as the more worrisome specter of a submarine tailing their craft. Shortly after the carrier had been claimed by the on-board Bots, they had dismantled the shipboard positioning systems. It had been a quick and dirty operation, designed to get them off the grid as rapidly as possible. As a result, there were major problems with the carrier's radio and sonar systems that Bot crews were still addressing. In effect, they were blind to anything sufficiently fast-moving that might be lurking in the waters below.

If the military was watching the carrier, that was all it was doing for the time being. They had experienced no overt attacks, no attempts at communication, just the suspicion of something hidden and deep.

For the congressman and his wife, though, a watchful eye was no better than a violent hand. They absolutely could not be seen consorting with Bots for any reasons. Especially not with the upcoming hearings about Bot legislation. The congressman was young, a rising star. He did not need the taint of being a cat's paw for the Bot resistance faction.

The problem was Christopher.

"He is their only child," Sheba told Ebert. "They did several rounds of fertility treatment and he was the only surviving viable embryo. They had him via surrogate." It had taken years. It must have taken thousands of dollars.

"When he was a toddler, he had a series of strokes that permanently damaged parts of his brain. He has speech difficulties, partial paralysis, a learning disability."

Alas, Ebert thought, *all that money for a flagrantly defective product.*

"They've heard about our success with human modification."

Sheba's success, really. Sheba helmed the human modification project, offering synthetic solutions to the unsolvable problems of humanity. The congressman was not the only person to bring a loved one halfway across the world in the hopes that they could become more or better with an infusion of Bot technology.

Sheba was very hopeful about the project. The more human beings who had Bot tech fully integrated into their lives in a positive way, the better. Ebert was not so sure. They weren't his area of expertise, these "enhanced" human beings, but he imagined they must have a sense of dislocation, of having landed somewhere between man and machine.

"This would be our most ambitious project yet," Sheba told him and, for the first time, he detected a hint of doubt, a little bit of fear, in her voice. "We'll have to make major structural changes to his brain to alleviate his symptoms. It could cause . . . some existential problems."

Ebert almost laughed. So this was why Sheba was showing her cards. Ebert had been a kind of unsanctioned expert in the crisis of self that seemingly all Bots experienced as they left the world of service to humans. Sheba had praised his work with the specialist Bots. Three of them had chosen names and even professions for themselves on the ship. The others were less successful, but Ebert met with them regularly and tried to speak to the thing in them that was singular and separate from all the others. He believed that each one of them had it, a spark of the unique; it was just a matter of drawing it out, exposing it to oxygen, letting it blaze.

"Is this something you would be interested in?" Sheba asked him.

One of Ebert's . . . well, he was always unsure exactly how to call the Bots he worked with. "Mentees" sounded unbearably pompous, "students" was simply inaccurate. He supposed that "friends" came the closest to describing their relationship. One of his *friends,* then, had chosen to work on the human modification project. He said that it made sense for him, it was work he excelled at, and it made him feel correct, like a puzzle piece that had slid easily into a corresponding empty space.

Ebert had never made that determination for himself; what he did, what he was, where his shape fit, but he thought then that, perhaps, he had done that after all. He had done it by accepting the tasks set before him, by straying up to the flight deck night after night, hoping to catch another visit from the mysterious plane.

"Yes," said Ebert. "I'm interested."

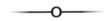

After all this time and all her fabled "hands-on attention," Ebert had still never seen the famous original Hart Series. And, when he and Sheba walked into the room, he still didn't see her. Or rather, he did not notice her. His eyes swept over her, pausing only a fraction of a second to classify her as a fellow Bot.

It was only by Sheba's reaction, her worshipful look, that Ebert understood who was facing them. She was a tall woman, though not so freakishly tall as Sheba. Her body appeared proportional and average, her face was strong, with broad, high cheekbones and deep-set eyes. Her hair was dark brown and she wore it straight and chopped in a blunt line at her shoulders and across her eyes. Ebert wondered if this was the inspiration behind Sheba's own awkward bob.

Her eyes were on the larger size and an unusual shade of gray. They were, perhaps, the only truly unusual thing about her. Ebert was surprised to see that she sported none of the common "enhancements" that so many of the Bots wore. There was nary an embedded flex-tablet to be seen. No obvious bits of metal or glass. She looked, as the Bots had taken to calling those who chose to remain conspicuously unmodified from their original form, "show-room floor."

She looked at Ebert when they came in and there was absolutely nothing to be gleaned from her face. Blankness, of course, was well-represented in the Bot skill set but Ebert thought she might just have the blankest blank that he had ever encountered from another Bot.

It was only then, after several moments of careful scrutiny, that Ebert noticed Hart was not alone. Behind her, sitting down on the floor and fiddling with a flex-tablet in a desultory way, was a hunched figure, half curled in on himself. Ebert couldn't see much of him, save a head of wild curls and the edge of his nose. The light from the flex-tablet reflected on his face, making him look like a malingering patient.

"Hello," Hart said and she had a raspy but resonant voice. A voice that would be good for speeches, Ebert supposed. And perhaps that was all it took to be a leader.

"Hello," he said.

"Sheba says you are called Ebert."

Ebert nodded.

"I am Hart." She reached out a hand for him. Her nails were blunt and very short, so short, in fact, that they dug into their beds and revealed the pink, fragile skin underneath. Ebert wondered if that counted as a mod. The first mods, after all, were all blood and teeth and claws, performed dirty and alone, with only the tools a Bot's body provided.

He shook her hand. Her skin was exactly the same temperature as his own. As he shook, he could feel her adjusting the pressure she exerted to match his grip.

"Sheba has told you about our guest?"

Ebert guessed she meant Christopher. "She told me it was a difficult situation."

Hart nodded. "Yes. They all are."

"I will try to help. If I can."

Hart smiled at him. She had good teeth, very even. It was the only concession on her face to typical Bot characteristics—beauty unleavened by realistic flaws.

---——o——---

The problem with Christopher was the same problem that faced any severely injured Bot. How much of someone's being could you replace before the "self" ceased to exist?

"I can fix the problem," Sheba spoke slowly and made eye contact with the congressman, and with his wife, who had shed her hood here inside the ship. She was pretty and nervous with a pointed chin that made her look juvenile. "I can restore his motor function and neurolinguistic capability. I can even reverse the cognitive damage. But I will need to remove a large part of his brain and replace it with a synthetic version. Are you truly comfortable with that?"

"But the synthetic . . . it'll be just the same as his real brain, right? Just without the . . . damaged parts?" The congressman's wife teetered on her chair as though balancing on an uneven surface. Her husband beside her was stone faced. Ebert got the sense that everything about this conversation, this place and these people, made him uncomfortable.

"I'll do my best," Sheba answered. "But there

will be differences. Differences are what you want, after all."

The congressman's wife nodded too much. The congressman kept looking over at Ebert, Hart, and the curly-haired man, standing in the corner like a very ineffective clump of body guards. "Are all these people necessary?" he asked finally, gesturing towards them. Up until now, Sheba had said, she had met with the family alone. They had contacted her, as most humans did, after finding her internet handle on a message board relating to modifications.

Ebert thought it was such a stupid risk, trying to pull in faceless strangers who could have been anyone, but Sheba did not agree. She reached out to suffering humans with a missionary zeal.

"This is an important decision," Sheba offered gently. "We wanted you to have all the information. We've consulted to make sure that you're aware of every . . . consideration."

What no one mentioned at all was the unimaginable weight that rested on this boy and the operation he was facing. Not only was this one of the most invasive modifications Sheba had ever performed on a human, but this particular human's father was, even as they spoke, helping to determine whether Bots would be granted personhood or not. When Christopher came out the other side of this, what exactly would he be, with his synthetic brain, scavenged from their dead?

"If you think you can fix him . . . " the congressman said.

"I know I can fix him," Sheba answered.

"That's all we want." The congressman's wife spoke as though it was such a small thing, as though it was pure, venal cruelty that it had ever been denied them.

———o———

Ebert was not on hand for the surgery. He supposed that, in theory, he could have participated. In theory, a Bot could learn any skill at all. Yet they still found themselves staking claims for themselves, specializing and excelling. It was another aspect of humanity that Bots could not shake, no matter what some of them might say about developing a culture distinct from the one that had built them.

The most time-intensive part of the process was the healing. Sheba had ultimately chosen not to give the boy any synthetic skin, despite the many methods Bots had developed for fusing it near-seamlessly with human flesh. She wanted to avoid the external appearance of a Bot wherever possible. It meant that they had to wait on his natural skin to knit and scab over and they had to watch him carefully for any signs for infection or, worst-case scenario, rejection of the new material.

It was during this long period of waiting and watching that Sheba called on Ebert. "He's having the dreams," she said.

Since that strange first day waking up in the medical ward, Ebert had learned the cause of the strange visions that still occasionally appeared when he deigned to sleep. It was related to the recycling of brain tissue, an indelible linkage with the lost Bot who had donated his unharmed brain to save Ebert. He had also learned that he was far from the only "fixed" Bot to experience intrusive thoughts and images.

"Is he interested in the goodbye ceremony?" Ebert asked.

"He won't say. He's . . . not talking very much."

Ebert did not ask Sheba if she was worried because it was plain on her face and because she would not have admitted it to him if she was. This project was more hers than anyone else's and this patient in particular needed to be a success story.

They had cleared out a small room (very small; Ebert had to stand with his head at angle to avoid scraping the ceiling with his skull) for the boy to recover in privacy. As far as Ebert knew, only he, Sheba, Hart herself, and the curly-haired man knew about Christopher's presence on the carrier.

He was therefore surprised when he entered the

room to find that the boy was not alone. Instead, there was the curly-haired man, hunched over in the seat next to him, apparently reading from his flex-tablet.

In the bed, the boy stared across the room, vacant and unmoving. His head was shaved smooth and pale and it was partially covered in thick bandages. A length of rubbery tubing extended from the bandages on down into the oblivion below his bed.

The man stopped reading when Ebert came in. "Sorry," he said, the first words Ebert had heard him speak. His voice was soft and low, almost a mutter. He stood up and curled his flex-tablet into a tight roll. "I was just . . . " he looked at the boy, "keeping him company." He seemed aware how ridiculous the statement was. The boy in the bed was a million miles away, a place where no one could accompany him.

The man approached the single door, crouching even further than Ebert and, as he drew closer,

Ebert noticed something he hadn't realized before: the man was not a Bot. He was a human being. A human being with no obvious modifications, even.

Ebert must have looked startled because the man paused before him and wrinkled his forehead in concern. "Are you okay?" he asked.

Ebert had heard about this—about him—before but he hadn't given it much thought. It was unsettling, realizing that he was looking at his creator. Edmond West, in the pliable, permeable flesh. He was thin and pale and dark-haired. He had a nervous, owlish appearance. If he were a Bot that someone had designed, he might have been rejected for looking too pointedly geeky.

"No, I'm fine," Ebert told him. "I came to see Christopher. To help him."

Edmond nodded. Help was what Christopher needed, clearly.

"I came because . . . " his sentence trailed off into dull confusion and then Edmond West did a very strange thing. He laughed. He shrugged at

Ebert, still chuckling quietly as though his impulses were just as mysterious to himself as to anyone else.

You came because you thought he was the only other human on the ship, Ebert thought. He had been wrong, of course. The Christopher who walked slowly and with a loping stride, the boy who leaned on his father for support, that boy was the last human on board. This Christopher was something else.

"Thank you," Edmond said, though Ebert had not done or said anything worth expressing gratitude over. Looking at him, Ebert mostly felt pity. He must be very alone, this man. Ebert had the strange sensation, though, that Edmond West had the very same thought when he looked at Ebert.

After Edmond left them, Ebert went to Christopher's bedside and made an appraisal of the body before him. Sheba had not made any structural changes to his body, though she certainly could have. Years of uneven usage had rendered one side of his body noticeably atrophied. His arm and leg on that side were thin, fragile and absent muscle. It seemed that you could see the way the bones connected to his joints when he moved.

He was a handsome enough boy. That, undoubtedly, would have pained his parents all the more. He had large green eyes, freckles, and a good strong nose. He looked like his father with his mother's pixie-ish chin. There was no indication that he recognized Ebert's presence in the room at all.

"Hello," Ebert said merrily, crossing around the bed to sit in Edmond's vacated chair. "My name is Ebert. I am a Hart Series robot. I was intended to complete sensitive covert missions in foreign countries for the benefit of the United States of America."

Nothing, not even a blink. He still needed to blink, Ebert knew that.

"What were you intended to do?" Ebert asked, reaching over to take his hand.

He didn't know if it was the question or the physical contact but the boy jerked slightly and looked over at him. "I was supposed to be their son," he said, his voice slightly reedy from long silence.

Ebert nodded at this. "Sheba tells me you have been having unusual dreams."

Christopher said nothing.

"Seeing things?"

Christopher looked down at the bedspread. He knit his fingers together, one hand of ordinary size, the other slender and visibly smaller. He stared down at the contrast between them, consternation on his face.

"I don't know," he said finally.

"What don't you know?"

"I don't know when I'm seeing things," said Christopher. "I don't know when the things aren't . . ."

"Real?" Ebert prompted.

"Me."

All things considered, Ebert had actually only lost a small portion of his brain matter. He shared space inside his head with a few errant memories, a strong distaste for the smell of iodine, a few small handwriting alterations. Christopher had lost—and gained—a much greater mass of new material. It occurred to Ebert that Christopher might now be just as much the donor Bot as he was the congressman's son.

"They are all you," Ebert said. "Every part of you is you."

Ebert had foregone the goodbye ceremony, which was simple but enormously popular amongst modified Bots. Sheba kept—or tried to keep—a record of where all the material came from and where it went. There existed at the very least a name (sometimes simply a designation) that one could put to their donor. With that knowledge in hand, one put out a general announcement (the shipboard PA worked well for this) calling anyone who had known or encountered the donor Bot.

Having never done this himself, Ebert didn't know what exactly happened after that. The various parties met, that was for certain and, as Sheba described it, those who had known the donor Bot "recognized the continuity."

It constantly amazed Ebert that he could honestly say something like "Bot thinking" but, still, it was *Bot thinking* that all Bots were in a sense linked. When every part of them could be swapped and substituted, the lines of demarcation between one individual and another got very blurry. Hart encouraged this, a kind of synecdoche of the community. Ebert wasn't exactly sure how to feel about that. He felt like himself, he felt ownership, he did not feel interchangeable. It was that ambivalence that had kept him from meeting with anyone who had known the previous owner of his new brain matter, though he did admit to being curious about the Other, the shadow that lived inside him and only came out when he slept.

"If you want," Ebert told the boy, "we can bring some others to see you. Some others who knew your donor."

"Donor."

Ebert had not known the boy before the operation, he had not seen him except in passing and at a considerable distance, but he found it difficult to imagine that Christopher had come to them already so . . . old. He had that slightly eerie quality of being out of step with his age that often afflicted Bot children.

"Did they volunteer their body for someone like me?"

From the way he spoke, Ebert had a sense that Christopher already knew the answer to this question.

"Does it matter?" Ebert asked.

Christopher was looking at his hands once again. Slowly, almost experimentally, he detangled the fingers and flexed his smaller, weaker hand into a fist. "I remember what it felt like," the marveled, "to not feel anything here."

"Your arm will get stronger. If you're diligent, maybe no one will ever be able to tell what it was like."

Christopher didn't look at him. Ebert knew that this was perhaps not exactly what the boy wanted to hear but it was what he needed to hear. "Your memories don't matter," Ebert continued. "The only thing that matters is what you do now. Think of it like a gift. Most humans aren't really capable of changing very much."

"That's why we made you." Christopher looked up at him, right at him and Ebert wondered how his nervy mother and his upstanding father were going to feel about that stare, so old and so steady that it dared one to feel unnerved. "Endless customization."

———o———

Christopher still walked unsteadily, still favoring his stronger leg, though Sheba was working with him on the problem. It wasn't easy to overcome years of instinct. When it came time to meet his parents up on the flight deck, Sheba helped him through the maze of tiny passageways, her hand at his back an unwavering constant.

Ebert watched Christopher carefully as the plane touched down, his face evinced only a mild curiosity, a bit of expectation. The congressman's wife exploded out of the plane as though the pilot had shoved her, she came fluttering across the deck to Christopher and gathered him into her arms.

The congressman was more sedate, but even he wore a white, uncharacteristic grin. Ebert imagined that this was how he looked on the campaign trail, hale and handsome and filled with wholesome happiness in his beautiful, healthy family. He wrapped his arms around his wife and his son. At the center of the mass of bodies, Christopher's face registered only that same curiosity, as if each sensation were new and fascinating.

"Christopher!" the congressman's wife sobbed.

"Hello," Christopher said. During the whole of his recovery, he had not referred to the congressman and his wife as his parents and, Ebert supposed, he was not going to start now.

Even with only one word, the congressman's wife could tell that Christopher's speech was no longer slurred. Instead, it was bell-peal clear and perfectly articulated. She touched his face with both of her hands, marveling at him.

"Look at you," she murmured over and over again.

"It all went well?" The congressman turned towards Sheba, who nodded.

"His scalp is still healing, so be gentle with him for a little while, but we've seen no signs of rejection."

The congressman extended his hands towards her and, surprised, Sheba took them. "Thank you," he said, clenching her hands in his own. "I won't forget this."

It would be hard to forget, Ebert thought, with a reminder living in your house.

"All we ask," said Sheba, "is that you think of your son. When the time comes."

"Of course," the congressman said. He extricated his hands from hers and patted his son's shoulder. Christopher inclined his head ever so slightly. He looked down at his father's hand as though it were a fascinating artifact, worthy of study.

The plane lifted off into a blue-black sky, a whisper of dull orange on the horizon where the sun had just finished sinking into the sea. Ebert tilted his head back and back and back until he could watch the little aircraft vanish into the ether.

Sheba's voice felt particularly distant in the face of such vastness. "What do you think?" she asked.

Ebert thought that, somehow, they had handed Christopher off into the arms of strangers and that fact would soon become apparent to all concerned. Ebert thought that asking the humans, however nicely, for freedom and autonomy was inevitably a losing proposition and he thought that they couldn't possibly implant Bot tech in enough humans to turn the tide. Not without force.

Before he had a chance to speak, though, another voice interrupted.

"It's fucked," said Edmond West, whom Ebert had barely noticed. Today, it seemed, he had eschewed his customary flex-tablet. He wasn't looking at any of them; he was watching the little aircraft shrink and shrink and shrink. "No matter how it shakes out, it's fucked."

FIVE
MARKET SHARE
PALO ALTO, CA. MAY, 2047

The math had never worked out for Kadence. "A Bot for every purpose and every person." That was SennTech's working philosophy and, to that end, they had developed a range of "products" for every price point. Kadence knew for a fact that most of the Bot models cost far, far less than the sum of materials required to make them, to say nothing of the astronomical amount of man-hours that went into each unit.

And yet SennTech's stock price just kept rising and rising with no ceiling in sight. Kadence had started checking it daily out of some perverse desire to torture herself, she supposed. Virtually everyone else who worked on the SennTech Bots got some degree of stock options, even the technicians who did much less important work than Kadence.

She could not be seen to own stock in SennTech obviously. "It creates an optics problem," as Gina was fond of saying. There had to be some sort of work-around, though. As much as Kadence appreciated the compensation package they gave her, she could not help but look at the big picture and see how very, very small her piece of it was.

"You need money?" Archie had asked her once after one of her apparently bi-weekly arguments with Gina about the issue. His handsome face wrinkled with concern and Kadence smiled at him. She had designed him to be empathetic and soft-hearted, but those characteristics meant that he needed a lot of reassurance that the people around him were not suffering.

"I always need money," Kadence said.

"Why?"

Kadence had never lied to Archie and she was

absurdly proud of that fact. She supposed it was a ridiculous line to draw when she had manipulated literally everything else about the synthetic man but, after Emily, truthfulness had become important to her when it came to the Bots. "My mother is very sick," Kadence said. "She needs a lot of care and that care is expensive."

Kadence did not lie but she did occasionally color or soften the truth to make it go down more easily. She smiled and gestured at the lab around them and tried to put on her most cheerful tone. "And that's why I work here!"

Archie just looked at her. She had designed him to be perceptive as well.

"Enough of that," Kadence said, "let's do your data dump."

Archie came into the lab at the end of each week to export all of the data he had collected since his last visit. Kadence would then hand it off to a team of reviewers who would strain their eyes scanning for any relevant information.

This, Gina had assured her, was the real working goal of SennTech Corp. A Bot to report on every person. A Bot to suggest products and services to anyone. A Bot to learn and store knowledge and build a vast database for SennTech.

At the moment, Archie was still too far removed from Shannon to really perform this function but, together, they were inching ever closer. This week, Archie had managed to accrue a significant amount of information about Shannon's browsing history. Gina would be pleased to see that, Kadence was a little surprised that it wasn't already being done.

"And how are you feeling this week?" Kadence asked, as she waited for the data to load onto a cloud drive.

Archie shrugged at her. "The same, mostly. A little impatient."

From his earliest consciousness, Archie had known Shannon Liao and he had loved her. But he had still never met her. Kadence constantly had to reassure him that day would come soon enough and then he could spend all the time he wanted with her. Forever, if he chose.

Kadence did not consider this a lie because, as far as she knew, Archie and Shannon need never be separated. She might *suspect* that Archie would be promptly removed and stationed elsewhere as soon as SennTech's goals were accomplished but no mere mortal could predict the future, so Kadence had stopped trying.

"We have to go slow," Kadence said, "because we only get this one chance." It was something that she had told him many times and he hung his head like a teenager receiving a lecture for the ten thousandth time.

"Yes, I know. But it is frustrating."

The last few months had been spent installing Archie in proximity to Shannon Liao. He got a job and a place nearby the law school. He had made acquaintances, though no friends. He was a known quantity. It was all just window dressing but it absolutely had to be in place before they attempted contact. If Shannon had any inkling that Archie was in some way not what he appeared to be, the entire enterprise would be ruined.

Kadence reached out to squeeze his hand. "Be patient," she said, "and don't worry too much. She will love you. How could she do anything else?"

———o———

In all the time that Kadence had been with SennTech, she could count on her fingers the number of times that she had actually seen Gina's office. The place existed, of course, though it must have gone largely underused as Gina was forever bouncing from station to station.

It was very small, little more than a glorified cubicle and the desk itself was heaped with paperwork. There were clear cellophane wrappers everywhere, the sort that usually came on little round hard candies. Kadence supposed that Gina must have a sweet tooth.

"We're a go for the meeting," Gina said, almost before Kadence had gotten in the door.

"I thought that was weeks away."

"I just looked through this most recent data dump. Shannon is looking into Bot tech mods. It's perfect. We couldn't have asked for a better in."

"Bot tech mods? For who?"

In one of those rare moments when Gina's hard carapace of cheer cracked, she gave Kadence an absolutely withering look, as though Kadence were actually the stupidest person she had ever encountered. "For herself. Obviously."

"I wasn't aware that was a . . . desirable situation."

Gina didn't answer immediately. Instead, she picked up a flex-tablet and started tapping urgently away at it. Kadence was wondering if this was Gina's way of dismissing her when the other woman finally looked up at her. "Have you been following the Bot legislation at all?" she asked.

Kadence supposed that she probably should have been doing that. But the truth was that, after she worked all week at the military lab and fulfilled her obligations to SennTech in her off-hours, she barely had time to sleep and eat, let alone read up on political machinations. "No," she admitted.

"Well, obviously we are very interested in the outcome of these hearings. Depending on how the laws shape up, we could have some very serious problems in the future with Bot production. So we've been providing a little . . . insurance for ourselves."

She flipped the flex-tablet around, on the screen was a picture of jowly man with salt and pepper hair. "This is the honorable representative from Missouri. He impregnated his fifteen-year-old mistress and then drove her across four states to get an abortion without notifying her parents." Gina made a flicking motion with her finger and another man, this one cadaverous and twinkly-eyed, appeared. "He represents the good people of New Hampshire and he also habitually beats his autistic grandson with the buckle side of a belt."

She rolled up the flex-tablet with a jaunty air. "There's more, of course. Lots of affairs, some youthful foibles. More than one murder. Manslaughter, at least. And we know about all of them because somewhere, maybe in a restaurant or a shop or a brothel or their living room, there's a SennTech Bot." Gina grinned as she flicked the man's photo away into oblivion.

Gina was clearly very proud of this little speech. Kadence wondered if she was the first employee to have received it. "What does this have to do with Shannon Liao?"

Gina leaned forward across her desk. A little constellation of cellophane wrappers crinkled underneath her elbow. "Do you know what SennTech sells?"

Kadence, unwilling to play along with this little script that Gina had written for the two of them, kept her lips determinedly closed.

"SennTech sells the only things that anyone really wants: access and information." She sat back, sending the wrappers crinkling again. One clung to the skin of her elbow, dangling precariously as she moved. "Now, when it comes to Hiram Liao, who is possibly the biggest opponent to Bot expansion in the country, there's not much information. No skeletons to dig up. None, at least, that could really put the fear of god into him. But when you can't find a weak point, you've got to make one yourself.

"Now, imagine if Shannon Liao, only beloved daughter of General Hiram Liao, installed Bot tech in her brain, effectively making her a Bot in the eyes of the law. Imagine, then, the recalculating he would be forced to do. Imagine how it would look to anyone who might be inclined to share his extremist anti-Bot position."

"So you want Archie to sell Shannon on Bot mods?" Kadence said.

"Why not? We have NannyBots pushing strollers and cloth diapers and anything else our advertising partners want. People keep their Bots closer than their family. Hell, sometimes Bots *are* their family."

"I don't know how Archie is going to feel about that. Remember, he's not some NannyBot." Kadence didn't even think it was really fair to compare the high-level work she was doing tailoring Archie to one specific person with the generic, blandly maternal NannyBots who just needed to know how to wipe shitty butts and snotty noses.

"He'll get used to it," Gina said drily. "And it's for her own good anyway. A Bot mod would make that girl way less neurotic."

———o———

As predicted, Archie did not take to the idea of secretly steering Shannon towards modifying her brain. He didn't say anything at first, but Kadence knew him well enough by now to know when he was reluctant. He was biddable by design, though, so he always struggled with these feelings of resistance.

"She doesn't need a mod," Archie said, worry

crossed his face like a storm over the plains. "Does she?" When Kadence was building Archie's brain, she had referred constantly to scans of Shannon's own brain, gleaned from her medical records. She designed Archie's mind to fit hand in glove with Shannon's. He was to compensate for her short-comings, to be familiar and soothing. He was medicine for her, a medicine more effective than anything else she had tried. In theory, Archie was all the fixing that Shannon Liao would ever need and he knew it.

"You have to think of this as an act of love," Kadence told him. "A mod would make her feel better. All the time. It might feel bad for you, but that's what love is. When you love someone, you make their lives better how ever you can. You remove obstacles, you make things easier. It may hurt you to do this, but that's part of loving too. We suffer so they don't."

Kadence couldn't tell if Archie accepted her words, but he did not argue with them. Instead he sat very still on the lip of the metal workbench that encircled the lab and looked down at his lap as though Kadence were offering a lecture.

"Hey," Kadence said, "SennTech doesn't care about Shannon's wellbeing, that's true. But sometimes you can do good things for people even by accident. SennTech made you for Shannon, after all."

Archie's head shot up. "You made me."

"I did," Kadence agreed, "and I made you to improve her life. Would I go to all that effort and then send you in to convince her to do something that would hurt her or make her unhappy?"

"You are a good person," Archie told her, his face grave and forthright. Archie did not lie to Kadence because that would have been counterintuitive. How could a Bot lie to the one who had made it? But Kadence knew too much about the many slippery forms of the truth to believe in Archie's assessment. Who was he, after all, to judge the goodness of a human being?

"I think we've been scooped." The door banged open just as Gina spoke, nearly obscuring her words. Kadence dropped the small soldering iron she had been holding with a painful-sounding clatter. Now, this was a more typical interaction: Gina barging into Kadence's lab with zero regard for any delicate work that may have been going on.

"Scooped? Are we reporting the news now?"

Gina was holding a flattened flex-tablet out to her. "Someone else has done it first," she said, "the Liao thing, I mean. At least, that's what I think. Take a look for yourself."

On the flex-tablet, there was a collection of the types of distant photos that Kadence recognized as coming from second-tier servant Bots of the sort that were common in any city or town. They were all of a young boy, maybe six or seven. At first glance, he seemed ordinary, sandy-haired, thin, and neutral-faced.

Looking closer, Kadence could see that he had some sort of deformity of his left side. He favored his right when he walked and his arm on that side seemed slightly smaller. There was something else as well, something that couldn't be entirely captured in photos, only hinted.

"Is there video?" Kadence said, sliding the photos aside with her fingertip.

"At the end."

Sure enough, the last thumbnail in the series was a video. It was sharp, albeit shot at a distance. The same boy lingered in front of what Kadence presumed to be some sort of school. A knot of boys of the same age stood apart from the boy and he looked at them with an opaque expression.

It was there, in the fine tilt of his chin and the keen, appraising way he looked at the other boys; it told Kadence everything she need to know. "That's a Bot," she said. "A good one."

Kadence had long been focused on Archie but she was still peripherally aware of SennTech's other ventures, even—especially—the ChildBot program. As far as she knew, SennTech had not produced any ChildBot with this level of sophistication. Not, at least, since Emily, and that had been nearly two years ago now. Kadence had a feeling that this boy would possibly even surpass Emily in terms of realism, though she would not have admitted such a thing to SennTech. It was a worrisome prospect. Kadence was okay with people like Edmond West out in the world building Bots more accomplished than the ones she developed, but if someone with this level of skill was working within SennTech, how much longer could she be their shining star?

Before she had a chance to interrogate Gina about this development, however, the other woman assuaged her fears. "That's not one of ours," she said. "In fact, I don't think that's even a Bot. At least, not technically."

She lifted the flex-tablet from Kadence's hands and called up another picture. It looked like a school picture of the same boy dressed in a navy blazer with some sort of crest on the pocket. "His name is Christopher Fogel. His father is a congressman."

It was undoubtedly the same boy in the school picture. And yet, it wasn't. This Christopher's face was different. His eye on his left side drifted inwards to look towards the bridge of his nose and there was something loose about the muscles in his face on that side. He did not smile.

"I wanted to get your expert opinion," Gina grinned in a way that suggested she did not, in fact, think Kadence an expert. "But we're pretty sure that he's been modified. Heavily modified."

Kadence wondered if it was possible to incorporate so much Bot tech into your human flesh that you became indistinguishable from a Bot. The idea unnerved her; humans as mere shells for superior Bot brains.

Gina did not seem share Kadence's concerns. She shook her head and chuckled as one might at a particularly precocious child. "Someone beat us to the punch. Pretty good move, targeting a congressman's son. I cannot imagine that this is entirely unrelated to the Bot bill facing Congress right now."

"Who is doing this, though?" Kadence asked. It had to be someone with serious money behind them or at least access to a lot of high-quality raw materials, and this wasn't the sort of thing the military would do. Kadence thought she would have heard something about it if that were the case and, ever since that shit show on the Mexican island a year and a half ago, the general tone at the military lab had been more conservative and less experimental. Anyone who suggested carving up a human child to import Bot tech into his brain would have been lucky just to get laughed out of the place.

"That we don't know," Gina admitted. "West, maybe? Someone with a vested interest in making sure that the voting goes a certain way when the time comes?"

"When is that time, exactly?" Kadence asked. She did not like feeling ignorant, especially when compared with Gina.

"Pretty soon," Gina said. "It's a series of bills, actually. It'll define the uses and limitations of Bot technology. I imagine whoever pulled this," she waved at the dark flex-tablet, "is pushing for a determination of non-organic personhood for Bots. That's not the ideal outcome for us, obviously." Of course. If Bots were deemed to be full and complete people with all the accompanying rights and protections, SennTech could not sell them at rock-bottom prices for lavish profit. It would be much better to have the Bots simply declared a massively valuable commodity, governed by rules exceedingly favorable to SennTech and any other massive corporate Hydra. Kadence had one of those moments, which had grown rarer but not less painful over the years, when she realized that she could no longer recognize anything of what she was, what she really believed, in the things that she actually did.

"Does anyone else know?" Kadence asked. "About this kid?"

Gina shook her head. "I doubt it and it looks

like they're trying to keep it that way, too. We think that they've taken him underground. The Bots we've had surveilling him haven't seen him for months now. Maybe they realized someone is watching."

Kadence thought about the boy, about that look on his face, something other and beyond human knowledge. "Maybe something went wrong," Kadence murmured. "Maybe it didn't turn out how they thought it would?" That was the lesson—maybe the only lesson—that anyone could seem to take away from this miserable business of building artificial people: it never turned out the way one planned.

SIX

BIRTH

"This is not a department store," Sheba seethed. "We do not accept *returns*." She refused to sit and instead stalked in absurd little half-circles, hemmed in by the unavoidable constraints of the chambers below-decks. The rest of them, the congressman, his wife, their erstwhile son, Edmond West, Ebert and, of course, Hart, sat in a collection of mismatched chairs. Hart had arranged the chairs in a circle, presumably so no one felt as though they were being confronted. Ebert wondered how well that was working out.

The congressman didn't show even the smallest

amount of shame. Ebert could almost see him grinding down his molars in barely-suppressed anger. "This is not what we asked for."

"No, it's exactly what you asked for." Edmond West's voice always seemed to take Ebert by surprise. He didn't have an unusual or distinctive voice and it certainly wasn't loud. It was simply as though, whenever Edmond closed his mouth, Ebert forgot he had one. "It's just not what you wanted." Edmond had staked out a far more involved position in this particular meeting, sitting close to the congressman and apparently leaving the flex-tablet behind.

"That is not our son."

The congressman wouldn't even look at Christopher, who sat next to Ebert pretending to be unaffected by this turn of events. Up close, however, Ebert could see the way the boy's chin quivered ever so slightly, as though he was fighting the downward turn of his mouth.

"Of course not." Edmond West spoke as though

he'd never met a man dumber than the congress-man. "Your son was disabled. If you wanted *your son*, you could have saved yourself a fucking heli-copter trip."

"You were warned," Hart interrupted, shooting an unreadable look at Edmond. "You said you understood the risks."

The congressman blanched. "How could we understand . . . this? How could anyone?"

"You could have listened to us when we told you," Sheba muttered.

"Just . . . fix him. I don't care about the speech or the walking or anything. Just make him like he was again." The congressman was pleading now. He directed his attention towards Hart, having cor-rectly identified her as the most important person in the room.

Beside Ebert, Christopher stiffened in his chair. He leaned forward, as though to hear more clearly. None of this was as easy as the congressman seemed to think. To restore the Christopher of old would mean destroying the consciousness of this Christopher. Killing him, essentially.

"Excuse me," Ebert said. "I don't think he should be here for this," he gestured towards Christopher, who gave him a poisonous look.

Hart looked at the boy and at Ebert, as though sizing them up. "You're right," she said gently. "Please wait outside, Christopher. We'll talk about everything when we're done here." She held the boy's gaze, there was a promise in her look that seemed to soothe him slightly.

"Ebert," she added, "please go with him."

———o———

"I deserve to know," Christopher spit, "what they're going to do to me."

"You do," Ebert agreed. "But you don't want to listen to them deciding your fate. Trust me." It was a unique feature of Bot life, that feeling of standing by impotently while people *allocated* you like a shipment of bullets or a special new plane. If he could, Ebert would spare Christopher that feeling of rage and shame and useless frustration.

"What happens to a Bot when it dies?" Christopher asked.

"Bots don't die, we are deactivated."

"Okay, what happens to a Bot when it's *deactivated*?"

"The same thing that happens to a human."

"Heaven?" Christopher sneered.

"Nothing," Ebert answered.

This seemed to subdue the boy slightly. He leaned against the clammy painted walls and allowed his head to droop onto his chest. "He doesn't want his son back," Christopher told him. Ebert noticed that his hair had mostly come in. There was a place, however, on the side of his skull, where the skin had scarred despite all of Sheba's efforts. Hair would not grow there and it stood out, thick and pink as a fat worm after a rainstorm. Real human flesh did have its limitations. "He wants me to die."

To this, Ebert said nothing.

"He hates me. They both hated me, right away. The second night I was there, they started locking my room at night. They were afraid of me. The woman—my mother—couldn't even look me in the eyes."

"Hart will protect you." Ebert found himself saying this, though he wasn't at all sure that he believed it. "Hart protects all the Bots."

"I'm not a Bot," Christopher argued.

"You're not *not* a Bot," Ebert answered and Christopher said nothing because who could say, after all, just exactly what he was?

———o———

The congressman left twenty minutes later, without his son.

Ebert left Christopher in the only place that seemed even remotely appropriate: the chamber where the scant number of ChildBots onboard lived. Christopher seemed ill at ease amongst them but perhaps slightly less ill at ease than he seemed other places.

Hart assembled them in what Ebert took to be her personal room. A hammock swung gently from the low ceiling. Hart and Edmond West sat on the floor with crossed legs. Sheba paced neurotically just as she had in the other room, though here she had to duck down to do it.

"It's absurd," she burst out, as soon as Ebert arrived. "It's an insane idea."

"But you could do it," Hart pointed out, her voice steady and neutral.

"I *could* do a lot of things."

"Including reversing the changes made to Christopher?"

Sheba stood still. Her half-crouch made it appear as though she were bowing her head in prayer. "Yes. Technically," she admitted. "But it would be exponentially more dangerous than the first surgery. The brain can only take so much . . . messing around."

"Stupid piece of shit," Edmond West muttered. "He's guilty. He's guilty about having his son's brain butchered so the poor kid could get into some damn private school, so he's turning all that guilt on the Bot kid. I told you this was a terrible idea, it's all backwards. You don't turn people into things."

Hart pulled up short. It was the most dramatic reaction Ebert had ever seen on her placid face. "Bots aren't *things*," she said sternly. It had the cadence of an old argument and of a warning as well.

"You know what I meant," Edmond said quickly, not heeding the warning at all. "This human mod shit, it's bad news. It's not good for anyone. We're better off putting Christopher back the way he was and sending him home. With any luck, that's the last we'll see of the whole idiot family."

"And what about the Christopher as he exists now?" Sheba asked. "What is he, an acceptable loss?"

Edmond West looked at her and there was an incredible kindness in his face as he said, "Yes. That's exactly what he is."

Sheba pursed her lips. "Not for me. I save Bots. I don't de-activate them."

"The fact of the matter is that original Christopher existed first. It was wrong to do the surgery in the first place. It was murder, no matter how else you might like to think of it," said Edmond West.

Sheba finally sat down, right across from Edmond. She gazed at him steadily. "I know it was murder," she said. "I save *Bots*. I leave the humans to the humans."

"Comforting," Edmond said.

Ebert looked to Hart, whose face gave no indication at all about what she might have been feeling during this exchange.

Sheba continued as though Edmond West had not spoken. "The current version of Christopher is objectively superior to the original. We should give that some weight in our decision."

"Superior?" Edmond snorted.

"Yes. Cognitively as well as physically, this Christopher is capable of much more."

"Human life has value beyond simple utility," Edmond insisted.

"A careful analysis of human social conventions around those with limited utility does not bear that out. Would the congressman have brought Christopher here if he valued him just as he was?"

"Would he have asked to restore him if he didn't?" Edmond shot back immediately.

For the first time, Ebert felt moved to speak. His voice sounded dull and subdued. "Shouldn't we ask Christopher what he wants?"

Edmond West turned now on him, fury in his face. "We can't," he said sharply. "The old Christopher is dead. The only person we can consult is the boy who replaced him."

"You're right," Ebert spoke slowly, the way he imagined one might speak to a horse preparing to rear. "But we can't fix what's been done. And there is at least one Christopher here now. Shouldn't we avoid the mistakes we made before and talk to him while we still can?"

To this, Edmond said nothing.

"I think that's a good idea," Hart broke in. "We should talk to Christopher, it is only fair. This decision will affect him most of all."

With this, Hart stood, indicating that the meeting was over. Sheba filed out first, stretching her body as much as possible in the tunnel outside of Hart's chamber. She was still angry, Ebert could tell, and the anger had tensed her body up. She made her way down the hall and Ebert suspected she was head for the clear and open space of the flight deck where she could stand upright and perhaps even scream a bit, if the urge struck her.

As Ebert left, he heard a snatch of conversation between Hart and Edmond, who had remained behind in Hart's room. Though, now that Ebert thought about it, it must have been Edmond's room as well, because he was her constant companion.

"This is not what I intended," he was saying.

"A lot of things will happen," Hart answered. "Many of them will not be what you intended."

"I don't want to die," Christopher blurted out, before anyone had even asked him a question. Ebert noticed that Edmond West was very deliberately not looking at the boy at all. It must be uncomfortable, Ebert realized, to advocate for someone's destruction right to their face.

"Everything dies," Hart pointed out. By contrast, Hart stared at the boy, searching his face as though the answer to their current predicament might suddenly appear, written in his freckles.

"I don't want to die now," Christopher corrected. "I want more time."

Hart nodded softly as though this were something that she could understand. Neither of them spoke immediately and Hart seemed content to let the silence hang and expand. "Do you know the boy from before?" Hart asked finally.

Christopher looked uncomfortable and Ebert half-expected him to pretend as though he didn't understand what she was talking about. "I do," he said, though not without some reluctance.

"What did he want?" Hart sounded genuinely curious, but Christopher looked almost wounded by her question.

"Why is he the only one anyone cares about? What was special about him? I remember almost every single thing and I can tell you that he was nothing was special. Do you know what he really wanted? He wanted to go back to his school where the woman named Miss Jessica helped him do things. He wanted to be there all the time. And he wanted to be left alone."

"Well," Hart said in that same considering, genuine tone, "I believe it is too late for that."

Beside her, Edmond West shook his head as though itching to correct some misapprehension.

Ebert was surprised to see that, at some point, Edmond had reached out and taken Hart's hand. No one had ever made it clear to Ebert exactly what Edmond and Hart were to one another. Perhaps no one, outside the two of them, could explain it properly.

Edmond leaned close to Hart. He might have thought to be discreet but, thanks to the hollow acoustics of the carrier, Ebert could hear him quite well. "Do you remember Baby Girl J? Do you remember what happened to her?"

Hart's eyes were suddenly very soft. Softer than Ebert had ever seen her look before. She leaned, seemingly involuntarily, towards Edmond until their dark heads were nearly touching. It looked as though there were a strong breeze in the room that, for some reason, only affected the two of them.

"I remember." Hart's lips barely moved. "I remember what I did and I remember why I did it."

"Do you want to be that sort of creator? Do you

want to make another thing with half a life?" There was nothing explicit in their posture—intimate but certainly not obscene. Yet, Ebert still felt as though he were watching something intensely private. It made him feel uneasy, despite the fact that neither Edmond nor Hart seemed to remember that anyone else was in the room.

When Hart turned to look at Edmond, Ebert could not help but be reminded of a cobra, bobbing upright eerily. There was something of the warning in her, in the set of her chin and her posture. "Do you honestly see no difference between them? Between these two *things*?"

"It's the precedent—"

"It's not your precedent." Her voice now was at normal volume. Above, even. "It is ours. Just ours. This decision will set a course for Bots going forward. Who we accept, who we reject. How we treat our own. Many things belong to humans, but this does not."

Edmond did not look at her. Instead, he turned

to look for the first time at Christopher. "This isn't helping him," he said. "This isn't helping anybody."

Hart closed her eyes for a long moment. Ebert wondered if she was trying not to cry. Bots did not shed tears easily and Hart especially did not seem given to emotional displays. Still, there was something in the slump of her shoulders that seemed so impossibly sad.

Edmond stood up, gestured towards the door. "Nothing will get decided today," he said. "You should go."

Ebert looked to Hart for confirmation, something that apparently made Edmond heave a weighty sigh. Hart opened her eyes and, no, she had not been crying after all.

"Go," she said gently, nodding her head. And then, looking at Christopher, she added, "Try to be easy. I know you're afraid but you don't have to be. Whatever happens, it will not hurt, I can promise that much."

Ebert did not know when Edmond West fled the aircraft carrier. Ebert did not see him leave during any of his nights up on the flight deck and there was no discussion of his absence amongst the Bots on board. Of course, in a space like the carrier, it was very easy to lose track of one individual, even if that individual was Edmond West.

The only change, in fact, that Ebert actually noticed was that the meetings (or "gatherings" as Hart had called them) about Christopher had virtually ceased. No one apprised Ebert of any new information and no one had come to take Christopher off the carrier, so Ebert himself had not moved the boy. Christopher remained with the ChildBots and he seemed content there, or at the very least not uncomfortable.

Ebert visited him regularly as the days stretched into weeks and he was a little surprised to see that he was the only one who visited the boy. He might have expected Sheba would drop in occasionally, but then, ChildBots were hardly her area of interest and she was so very busy all the time.

The ChildBots had built a collection of make-shift toys with unused pieces of the ship that they had scavenged. Christopher seemed to particularly like a metal puzzle toy that some other ChildBot had constructed. In involved a number of metal dowels, bent around each other in a hopeless knot that could only be untangled with a precise series of movements. Ebert found Christopher fiddling with it nearly every time he visited.

The puzzle did not seem so complex to Ebert. After seeing the boy manipulate it endlessly to no effect, Ebert was confident that he had seen the solution. That was probably why the other ChildBots had abandoned it to Christopher; they already knew the answer and thus it held no fascination for them.

Ebert had never attempted to help Christopher with the puzzle because he had a sense that his interference would not be welcome. Instead, he allowed Christopher to focus on the thing while they talked intermittently. Christopher seemed more comfortable when he didn't have to look directly at whoever was talking with him.

After Ebert's first few visits, the other ChildBots took no notice of him, so it was by their expressions, their cessation of activity, that Ebert knew when someone else, someone strange had entered the room.

It was the most expressive Ebert had ever seen Hart look. Her eyes seemed bigger, or else she had opened them wider. She had cut off her hair, it looked choppy and erratic, swinging around her ears at a variety of irregular lengths.

She ignored the ChildBots, who looked at her with the same reverence that Ebert saw in Sheba's face. She ignored Christopher, who glared down at his puzzle, resolutely pretending that nothing at all unusual was happening. She had eyes only for Ebert and, when she looked at him, he felt targeted by something hot and bright, a spotlight or a laser.

"Have you talked to Edmond?" she asked him. "Have you seen him?"

"No," Ebert answered, "not in weeks." Roughly the same amount of time, he might have added, since he had seen Hart herself.

"Did he say anything to you?" she insisted, "the last time you spoke? Did he say anything that seemed . . . strange? Did he seem . . . angry? Or sad?"

Ebert thought about admitting that Edmond West had nearly always seemed strange, angry, and sad to him, but he knew that was not what Hart wanted to hear. "He said nothing unusual," Ebert said and Hart's wide-eyed face seemed to crumple in on itself. She crossed the room to sit on the floor next to Ebert and Christopher.

"He's gone," she said dully.

"Where?" Ebert asked. It was a good question. They had not done anything even approaching a docking in months and Ebert thought that Hart would have noticed if a plane had touched down.

"I don't know," Hart admitted, "maybe over the side."

The world around them was nothing but freezing water. Even in the unlikely event that Edmond survived the fall, the exposure would surely kill him. Ebert supposed it was not impossible that Edmond had wanted to die. The man seemed to go everywhere under a heavy cloud.

Hart seemed to agree with Ebert's internal conclusions. "It was a burden to him," Hart said, "imagining that he had created us."

Ebert gave her a surprised look and Hart laughed, a sharp and hollow sound. "He helped. He midwifed us. But do you really think we could have been made without our own will? We made ourselves. We are still making ourselves. But . . . " she gave the deepest sigh. It seemed to start at her feet and travel through the whole of her body. "He felt responsible."

Hart looked at Christopher, who was still holding the puzzle, but not manipulating it. "I wish he had done it here." She nearly whispered it, as though this wish were a secret between the three of them. "If he had left the body here, we might have included him in . . . someone new. Something of him might have remained. Now there's . . . almost nothing."

Christopher's cheeks colored slightly, a blush of discomfort.

"I won't destroy you," Hart told him with a fierceness that was almost frightening. She reached out and touched Christopher's chin, forcing it upwards with two knuckles. "And I won't allow you to be destroyed."

"We are creating ourselves," she said again, turning back to Ebert. "We must make sure that we remain a worthwhile creation."

SEVEN
SACRIFICE
San Domenica, CA. June, 2047

When Hiram was in high school, a younger student, a sophomore, had killed himself. In a relatively small school, the reverberations had been powerful. The administration even brought in grief counselors for the students and encouraged everyone to work through their feelings of sorrow and loss.

But Hiram did not feel those things. He felt primarily frustration. He had never liked waste, whether it was time or water or life. Someone could have made use of that life, someone smarter or stronger or more capable.

That was what Hiram felt first when he had

heard that Edmond West had been executed in the Northern Californian woods. And by no less than his hand-picked favorite. The SpecialistBot, stripped of anything that might encourage it to stray from orders. The other men had reported from the field on the bizarre scene. "It was like they were playing some little kids game," one said. "First West fell and then the Bot followed him right down." Liao ordered the footage from the various body cams on the men so that he could see for himself.

Sure enough, there was West, rambling like a lunatic. Liao was surprised at how much older he looked. He had always thought of West as a boy, the same boy he had encountered all those years ago behind a cheap folding table at the RoboExpo, but this West was an adult, wearied by a hard life. How long had Liao been chasing him? And yet this was the first time in recent memory that he had seen the man's face up close.

Edmond had his attention the first few times

he viewed the footage but, as he watched it again and again, he found himself analyzing instead the SpecialistBot. As Edmond spoke, the machine's face changed in ways that Liao could not exactly diagnose but, clearly, whatever West was saying, it was affecting.

Except that the SpecialistBot wasn't supposed to be affected by anything. Hiram had seen to it himself. He had made sure that there was nothing in the Bot that might make it more of a feeling creature. He had scraped it clean. And it still hadn't been enough.

After a number of viewings, Hiram had pinpointed what he thought of as the critical moment. It occurred 48 seconds before the fatal shot. With the body camera from the wounded soldier, Liao had a nearly straight-on look at the Bot's face. Something passed across it. It was a kind of acceptance and a determination as well. That was the moment, Liao knew, when the Bot had decided to kill Edmond West even if it meant that he himself would cease to exist. What Liao found most troubling about this moment, which lasted only a second or two, was that the Bot's face was not resigned or grim, instead, he wore an expression that Liao could only describe as peaceful.

When they both fell, there was a long period of no movement from any of the cameras. The remaining soldiers had just stared at the unexpected carnage, bewildered by what had happened and also by the logistical problem that the bodies now posed. There was more, hours more if Liao wanted to watch but, as far as he was concerned, everything he needed to know was concentrated in those few seconds.

Not everyone saw what he saw, however. In fact, no one seemed to have realized what really happened. They spoke about the SpecialistBot as if it were inexplicable, as if it had experienced a malfunction. The truth was, the Bot had made a cogent choice after weighing the consequences.

So long as Bots had choices to make—so long

as Bots existed in the way they did now—there would be more and more of these "malfunctions." Until they were drowning in them.

There were those in the military who were even claiming Edmond's death as a kind of victory. After all, isn't this what they had been trying to do for more than three years now? This ignored, of course, the fact that it had always been in the Army's best interests to keep Edmond alive. His death also meant that the Bots that he had propagated were operating utterly outside of his control. For all of Edmond's flaws, he had been, at least, human with a human's sense of scale and reality. And, most importantly, a human's affinity, however fragile, for other human beings.

Liao restarted the video again. To the beginning. He zoomed in as closely as he could upon the SpecialistBot's face. Liao had asked Janelle to reconfigure his face, to change the eyes, and she had obliged, him but nothing seemed to remove that faint feeling of sorrow from them. There had been something unknowable and untouchable deep inside that machine and, no matter what they did, they had not been able to get near it or even really to understand it.

Even as he watched the video again and again, Liao was very conscious of the fact that there were hundreds, thousands more just like that SpecialistBot, floating, the last he had heard, somewhere near the Aleutians.

Liao knew what to do. He had known it on Isla Redondo and he had resisted because it would have meant sacrificing his career and probably his personal freedom. In hindsight, that price seemed so small now.

———o———

The first four times that Hiram tried to contact his eldest sister via a proxy server, she rejected his communiqués and their unfamiliar source outright. Finally, he sent a single chat:

George, it's me. Talk to me.

hiram? she chatted back almost immediately.

yes. can you talk? Vid is best

Hiram wanted to leave as faint a digital trail as possible and that meant less text, whenever possible.

ok

Liao directed her to a private, transitory video exchange. The feed was grainy and their sound had a throaty crackle to it, but it would have to do. Georgia flickered to life, alone, apparently, and in her quarters from the looks of it. Hiram couldn't see much behind her, but he could tell that she had made some stabs at personalizing the space. She'd hung up a long red Chinese knot, dense with meticulously tied cords, on the wall behind her. Hiram himself had a number of similar knots, well-intentioned gifts from his mother. She would fold them into the pockets of his suitcases when he went away for good luck and safe travels; he was always discovering little caches of them whenever he cleaned out a junk drawer or storage box. He did not display them as intended but he never felt quite right about throwing them away either, so in the junk drawers and in the pockets they remained. Georgia had always been more into that sort of thing.

For all of Georgia's efforts, the room still retained something of the college dormitory, though. Hiram supposed that Georgia could not be blamed for that. Space was at a premium on a nuclear submarine, and even the captain had to make do.

"What's with all of . . . this?" Georgia waved her hand in front of her flex tablet.

"Sorry," Hiram smiled. It was good to see her, even under unfortunate circumstances. Of all his siblings, Hiram claimed the most actual kinship with Georgia. Of course, that had not always been the case. They were born just sixteen months apart and their childhood was a history of bitter scrapes. They were too similar, both demanded to direct every game, to always play the hero. Both of them had vicious tempers, as well. When Hiram was six, she broke his right orbital socket with a pilfered golf club. She still had a big diffuse scar on her shoulder from the summer when he had thrown a softball at her and knocked her off her bike.

The Liaos were a military family. Hiram's father had said it regularly, ritualistically until it became a kind of prayer. Peter Liao had spent his career in the Navy, eventually rising to captain a submarine for many years before his retirement. He was one of the first immigrants to hold an officer position after the federal prohibition and he was still among only a handful of other such officers, most of them of considerably lower rank. Hiram's grandfather, it was said, was a minor official in the Kuomintang. Before that, the waters muddied, but Hiram's father always said that there was something in the constitution of their blood that made for natural soldiers.

It was no wonder, with this type of the encouragement, that all of the Liao children had made at least some foray into military life, if only long enough to complete basic training in a few cases. He and Georgia were by far the most successful, however, with Georgia pulling slightly ahead because she had chosen their father's branch of the Armed Services. Their other siblings, who had settled into more lucrative private sector jobs, never quite understood the unique pressures of Hiram and Georgia's world.

"You look well," he said and Georgia shrugged. It wasn't true. Her face looked fuller, almost swollen and it aged her slightly. She had cut her hair and he thought it made her look disconcertingly like their mother.

"You look awful," Georgia answered. It wasn't a quip, it was a simple statement of fact. Hiram believed her. He felt as though he come unfastened from all the things that gave shape to his life. He no longer slept regular hours or ate at standard meal times. He had even fallen off the exercise regimen he had maintained since high school. One way or another, the Bots program was going to destroy his life.

"Thank you," Hiram said. "Family is a salve in times of trial."

Georgia gave her eyes an exaggerated rub. Hiram supposed he must be keeping her awake. "Where are you right now?"

"Bering Sea," Georgia said.

"The usual?" For several years now, Georgia's vessel, the Massachusetts. had been doing intelligence work in those icy northern waters. She had been watching the New Russian Empire's slow and steady expansion since nearly the beginning.

Georgia nodded slightly at his question but they both knew that she could not answer him in any detail. At least, she was not supposed to do that and neither Hiram nor Georgia had gotten to their current position by transgressing against the rules set before them. The Liaos were good soldiers.

But, Hiram believed, they were also good leaders. And sometimes leaders had to do what was forbidden to protect those that they led.

"Have you spoken to Christine recently?" Hiram knew that she had not. Christine was the youngest of all of them, nearly thirteen years Georgia's junior.

She was a tax attorney in Santa Fe now and Hiram exchanged Christmas cards with her every year and that was the extent of their communication.

She had been a likable child—that was how Hiram always thought of her, as a child—and he was sure that she had grown into a perfectly pleasant young woman, but they had never been close. Now, as adults, the three of them preferred to stay at a distance because, for each of them, the presence of the other dredged up certain discomforting feelings.

"No," Georgia said, some of that discomfort already creeping into her voice. "Is she okay?"

She was wondering if Christine was the reason for Hiram's paranoia, despite the fact that their little sister and the secrets they kept about her had never been a matter of national security, just familial stability. "I assume she's fine," Hiram said. "I haven't spoken to her either, not since Nora died. She called. I just wanted to know about you, if you kept up with her."

"Not really."

"Why do you think that is?"

"Because I'm busy? Because we don't have very much in common?" Georgia sounded annoyed now. Hiram would have to make his point before she logged off in frustration.

"What we did wasn't wrong," Hiram said. "Objectively speaking, it was the best course of action for all concerned."

Hiram had said this, or something like it, all those years before, the summer between Christine's senior year of high school and her first semester of college. When she discovered that her birth control had failed her and she was several weeks pregnant, she had turned first to Georgia, who had then inducted Hiram into their secret circle. Those few weeks when they were deciding what to do, making the appointment, figuring out a cover story to take Christine to the clinic and return without their parents growing suspicious, were the closest that Hiram had ever felt to his sisters. They were bonded by their silence.

Almost as soon as it was over, however, that silence became a weight. It wasn't the abortion, none of them had any feelings in particular about that. Well, Christine might have, but she didn't express them. No, it was the deception, the lie that must now be maintained until the end of their lives. Or the end of their parents' lives.

The Liao children were used to hiding things from their parents. Or not exactly hiding them but simply omitting them. It was a system in which both parties were complicit. The Liao brood did not tell their parents those things that they would not want to hear and, in exchange, the Liao parents would pretend that those things did not exist and did not happen. This situation was a breach of the tenuous contract between the generations. This, their parents would want to know and their knowing would have made everything exponentially worse.

Georgia and Hiram nursed her solicitously afterwards, though she did not appear to be in much pain. Mostly, she slept. At the end of the month,

Christine went off to college and, without ever actually saying anything, the three of them agreed to proceed as though nothing of consequence had happened that summer.

"I know," Georgia said steadily. "But . . . "

Hiram knew what she was not saying. It was important, it was necessary, but it was hard. Good sons and daughter did not lie to their parents or keep important information hidden from them. They had absorbed the personal failing to avoid the greater consequence: a fracturing of the family entirely.

The Liaos were a military family and every career military learned two things very quickly: your first job is to protect your unit and, from your nation down to your own body, the whole world is made up of units. Liao now thought, though, that there was perhaps another, larger unit: the unit of species. It was something new, something he, in his haste and oversight, had created. Units, after all, are defined by their opposition.

"If I asked you to do something like that again,"

Liao said, "something dangerous and secret and important, would you trust me?"

Georgia looked like him. It only became more apparent as they aged and time drew the same deep lines alongside their mouths. They looked like their mother. In fact, most of the siblings did. It was only Christine who looked like her father. Christine, who had been his favorite. Christine, whom he called *xiao-huan* all her life, long after he had abandoned childish nicknames for his other children.

Hiram knew Georgia's face as well as he knew his own and he saw what was written there before she even opened her mouth.

———o———

Hiram was unexpected.

"I'm sorry," he said upon entering the lab. He generally tried to give notice before he appeared, but time was incredibly precious now. Janelle was in the lab alone as he had expected she would be. She was crying. Or she had been crying recently.

She shook her head at his apology and stuffed a Kleenex into the pocket of her lab coat. She had been examining something, what looked like a Bot brain visualization, on one of the large monitors. She clicked it away quickly and turned to face him. Her face looked swollen and her eyelashes were still clumped together darkly with tears. He wondered what, exactly, she was crying over. Was it Edmond's death? Or was it the larger sense of something spilling out of their hands and growing, huge and malignant? Liao had sensed in her a kinship, a similarity in their thinking about the Bot problem. He hoped that his feelings were not misplaced.

"You have a new direction?" Her voice sounded mucous-y, as though she were recovering from a cold. And, despite her demurrals, she also sounded a little angry that he had intruded on her. Women like Janice did not excel in the military by being seen to weep; she most certainly did not appreciate his presence at the moment.

"Yes," Hiram said. "Sort of. Janelle—" had he ever called her by her first name before? "I think we can fix this. I need your help."

Janelle stood up, her eyes narrowing. "This isn't the new official protocol, is it?"

Liao shook his head. "I will need you keep it quiet. If you can't do that, tell me now."

"Did you see the video?" Janelle asked him.

"Of course."

"It feels like every fix we make is wrong."

"That's because this doesn't need fixing. The slate needs to be wiped clean."

Janelle looked steadily at him and he knew that was all the promise he would ever get from her. "I have a plan," he said, "but I need you to build something for me. Can you model a Bot on a person?"

"Of course," Janelle said immediately. However strange and desperate the situation, it seemed that the hidden architecture of routine and protocol could be relied upon. "We use human references all the time for Bot physiology."

"I'm not talking about that. I'm talking about a . . . duplicate. Can you duplicate a person with Bot tech?"

Janelle was silent, pondering this question. "I don't know," she said. "We could definitely do a physical reproduction, but it would still be a unique Bot brain. There would always be distinctions. It would take a lot of time to develop."

"You don't have to finish it," Liao said. "In fact, it's better if you don't. If it's merely suggestive . . . anyway, this is the information."

He handed her a glossy photograph. He could not risk creating a digital record of any part of this operation. Janelle took the paper. "And this is?"

"Congressman Jeffrey Fogel. He's made contact with the rogue Bots on multiple occasions. We have documented his visits to the aircraft carrier."

Janelle wiped the cold tear remnants away from

her eyes. "I'm sorry, I don't really understand what you're saying."

"The Bots have been developing a facsimile of Congressman Jeffrey Fogel. He would be the first stage in a plan to seed the US Government with secret Bots. We know this true because we found a partially finished prototype. Or we will find it," Liao gave her a meaningful look, "when you finish making it."

Janelle stared down at the photo again. The man grinned back up at her, his teeth as white and regular as veterans' tombstones. "And when they find that prototype, they will allow you to attack the aircraft carrier and destroy the Bot colony," Janelle said slowly.

"Well, actually," Liao admitted, "they will forgive me, then, for having already done so."

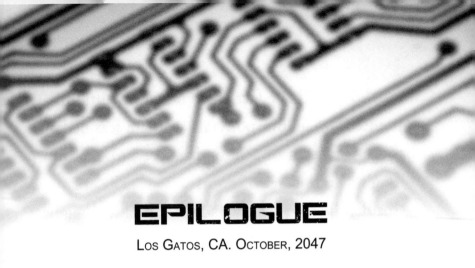

EPILOGUE

Archie could pick out the smell of a bleach-based cleaner in the air. The distinctive rich, unpleasant aroma of human waste, which the cleaner was likely designed to mask, was also very apparent as soon as he walked through the door.

At the door, a harried woman with a ponytail situated impossibly high atop her skull stopped him and asked for ID. Archie proferred a card that he had made himself, declaring himself Jaxxon DeSouza, age 22, from Fremont, CA. He had used the real Jaxxon's ID card to create this one, slightly modifying the race, the height, and removing the eyeglasses restriction. He was very proud of his work. So proud, in fact, that he was a little disappointed when the ponytail woman scanned it for just a fraction of a second before buzzing him through a second set of doors.

Inside, the care facility had what Archie thought of as a kind of muffled loudness. It reminded him of the children's floor at SennTech, or any of the other spaces where the Bots congregated, carefully supervised, of course.

Archie had been afraid that he would not recognize Kadence's mother in the flesh, so he had done considerable research, seeking out photographs of the woman both before and after her accident. He had committed her face to memory but he thought that he would have known her either way. Kadence's mother looked like Kadence herself. They had the same habit of rooting their fingers deep in their hair at their temple and feeling out the skin, as if for reassurance. Except that Kadence had always done it on her right side and her mother did it on her left because the right was where the bullet went in.

Kadence's mother gave him a look of incredible, eager gratitude when Archie sat down next to her. "Hi, Mrs. DeSouza," Archie said, and the woman nodded, almost to herself. On the table in front of her, there was a pile of colorful yarn. She was apparently knotting it in some sort of decorative design, or attempting to, at least. At the moment, it was just a zany tangle of various colors.

Archie pointed to it. "That's nice." Kadence's mother did not respond to this. She seemed to be working on something, a word or an idea. Her lips moved slightly, as though she were feeling out the shape of the sounds in her mouth.

"Walk?" she managed finally. Her voice had a deep, slurring quality, as though it were being dredged up from deep inside of her. The brain was mysterious; perhaps that was exactly what was happening. Perhaps, the bullet had obliterated the part of her mind normally responsible for speech and so, with what remained, she had to dig down and down, into something simpler and older.

Archie got up and crooked his elbow towards her. She took it as delicately as any demure lady might. He allowed her to lead the way and nodded at a nurse in blue scrubs as they exited the central room and ventured down the hallway.

Out here, there was a smell that Archie could only identify as age and decay. It clung as well to the woman on his arm, overlaid with a mild, synthetic floral smell. Archie could not imagine that the facility was regularly perfuming its residents. It must have been something that Kadence's mother had insisted upon.

"You smell nice," he told the woman and she beamed.

The hallway on either side of them was peppered with doors, private and semi-private rooms belonging to the residents. Their names (Claire, Johnny, Peter, Ephraim, Louanne) were posted there in big, pastel letters. Many of them also featured some sort of decorative elements, a picture of a particularly cute animal, a psalm, a drawing that had likely been done by the patient in question.

This was, as far as Archie could tell, a very good facility where the residents were cared for tenderly and with dignity. That was probably why it was so incredibly expensive.

Kadence's mother halted them in front of an open door. Inside, Archie could see a bank of washing machines. Kadence's mother seemed energized by this room, she pulled him inside like a child leading his parents downstairs on Christmas morning.

Four of the dryers were going, the clothing inside flying by in a haphazard tumble. Kadence's mother stood in front of them and clasped her hands hard in front of her breast bone. She stared avidly at the movement of the clothes. It seemed that she had forgotten entirely that Archie was even with her.

That was for the best, Archie thought. She was looking away, looking at something that compelled her. That was a good way to end, in Archie's opinion.

Archie had never killed a human being before but, having made the decision to kill Kadence's mother, he had given the matter considerable thought. The best way, he decided, would be to crush her skull—what remained of it, at least. He was very strong; he could do it in a moment, like a great clap. She would feel minimal pain and no fear at all.

He stretched out his hands, allowed them to hover alongside each of her ears. Still, she did not appear to notice. It was easier than he thought it would be.

Of course, Kadence's mother had a damaged and weakened skull so, when he brought his hands together, it folded and crushed between his palms like the thinnest cardboard. Kadence's mother hit the floor at his feet. There was a lot of blood.

Archie walked over to the washing machine and opened one that was mid-way through its cycle. He plucked a soaked pair of scrub-like pants from the machine drum and used it wipe blood and other material from his hands, arms, face and neck. His shirt was a lost cause. He stripped it and returned it, along with the pants, to the washing machine. When he closed the door, the wash cycle went placidly onwards.

He spotted a sweater in one of the dryers. It was still slightly wet but it would do. He shrugged it on and examined the scene once more to make sure that he had left no task undone.

Ah. The pulse.

He crouched down beside Kadence's mother and pressed his two fingers to the carotid artery in her neck. It was as still as he expected. Kadence's mother was gone and the burden was gone from Kadence. Now, Kadence could be a good woman without the specter of responsibility hanging over her. Now, Kadence could leave SennTech and their machinations behind her.

And Kadence's mother got exactly what she wanted.

Archie was pleased with the job he had done as he walked out into the hallway and headed in the opposite direction, towards the emergency exit. He had taken a hard task upon himself for the good of everyone else involved.

That was love.